RENEGADE APACHE

E. C. HERBERT

Prologue

It is said that ten Indians with a good leader is a force to be dealt with, so when word got out that a small band of mixed breed Indians, led by a young warrior who was given the name of Many Lives, had attacked the Cooper homestead and savagely slaughtered its occupants, US Marshal Harry Finch was assigned the job to track him and his band of redskins down and bring them to justice.

Remembering an earlier associate who he had teamed up with was from Nebraska, Harry contacted the now, US Marshal Conrad Johnson who was delighted to have the chance to work with Harry once again.

Because of Harry's recommendations, Conrad was promoted to US Marshal and was given his own territory to be in charge over. He was well liked in the organization having proven himself over and over again as a top notch Marshal.

Being from Nebraska, he had kept up as much as he could on the conflict between the settlers and the Indians and the involvement of the military.

Many battles were fought in the Nebraska Territories which became known as the Great Sioux Wars. It saddened Conrad whenever he received news of those battles, even though he had been gone from that area for years, he considered it still to be his home.

And now, years later, he was going back and joining who he considered to be his mentor, Conrad figured it didn't get much better than that.

Boarding the train, Conrad would be in Omaha in one and a half days to meet Harry there and he was looking forward to it.

Meanwhile, Many Lives was sitting around a campfire with his braves. They were celebrating the successful raid on yet another settler's homestead, as a matter of fact one of the daughters was in their company, having been abducted in the raid. It was a typical practice to kill off the men folk and take their women to use until they all tired of them, then they would be killed.

Up until now, no soldiers had been able to capture Many Lives and his renegade followers. They had been close to capture on many occasions, but always managed to elude the soldiers and seemingly disappear into thin air, so the name Many Lives was given to this young Cheyenne brave.

Many Lives had vowed to never be captured alive and to kill as many of the white settlers as possible for taking their land and breaking all treaty agreements his father had once made with the government leaders.

Harry and Conrad's skills would be put to a test as they hunted down the elusive Many Lives and his band of RENEGADES….

Chapter 1

Harry was disturbed by the telegram he had received advising him of the massacre of the Cooper family by the band of renegade Indians led by the young brave who had been nick-named Many Lives.

They were a band of savages who had sworn never to be captured alive, and the Nebraska landscape was littered with dead soldiers and settlers to confirm that statement.

Many Lives, whose father was a chief of a small band of prairie Cheyenne Indians, wanted nothing more than to live on the land in peace with the white man, hunt some buffalo, and live out their existence bothering no one.

Many Lives had gone hunting with several of the younger braves the day their village was raided by the soldiers and everyone was killed including his father, mother, women and children. It made no difference to the white soldiers, that day.

They had done nothing to provoke this slaughter, but that was also true in several of the Indian village slaughters carried out by the government soldiers as they tried to control the Indians and take their land.

The settlers wanted the rich soil for themselves as they settled the land. They were headed to California to settle this free land the US Government staked them in return for occupying the land and making it productive.

The only problem being, it wasn't the government's land to give away. It was land belonging to the Native Americans and they weren't going to up and leave it without a fight.

The Battle of the Little Big Horn or Custer's Last Stand had taken place the year before Conrad and Harry were given the task of capturing one of the braves who had taken part in that battle. Many Lives had sat in the council of Sitting Bull, Two Moons, White Bull, Crazy Horse, and Chief Gall before that battle took place.

Many Lives was accustomed to the fight and had many scars to show for it. On several occasions, he had gone hand to hand with the foot soldiers who had been sent to capture him. Several times he walked away wounded but alive, leaving several soldiers lying dead with their hair attached to the cross the chest, ammo belts he had taken off one of those he had killed. Although he didn't use the white man's noise makers, as he preferred his trusted bow and arrow.

Next to Many Lives was his brother Twisted Knee.

Twisted Knee was given the name from his youth having been thrown from a horse and landed on his knee which twisted up behind his back, never healing properly so that he walked with a limp. Twisted Knee was a fine warrior as were the others who rode with Many Lives.

As the tribes of the prairies surrendered to the white soldiers and settled on reservations, Many Lives and his warriors refused to give up and succumb to the White Man's ways. They chose to be defiant and fight back, not only against the soldiers, but also those settlers who stole their land. What had started out as a band of warriors who raided, burned, and raped the settler's womenfolk, had long since escalated into killing them and removing their scalps, a practice that was not highly looked upon by the white folks.

Many Lives had fought alongside many great chiefs in the past and had learned to be elusive and could cover his tracks, or expose them to lure you into a trap, which he would spring with great success. He had many scars to show for the fifty-seven scalps he wore tied to his ammo belts. Some say they captured any bullets that entered them preventing anyone from killing him.

Many Lives was convinced he couldn't be killed by any white man's bullets which made him a much more deadly Indian. He was shot at least seven times by the white soldier's bullets at The Battle of the Little Big Horn. Given these stories, the band of renegades who rode with him were sure they had the same protection and became just as fearless as he was. Whatever this band of renegades did, they enjoyed much success and had never lost a life.

Many Lives had also been blessed at birth with the symbol of the Great Clan Bear who was said to have lived amongst his ancient relatives and continued to dwell with them today. One day when Many Lives was in his youth, he met up face to face with the Great Clan Bear and stared him down. Finally winning out on the staring contest, the bear turned and went back up the trail it had come in on.

Many Lives told this story on many occasions while sitting around the campfire with his band of braves and each time he told it, he grew in stature until he towered over the bear. Not only were these stories told by Many Lives to his braves, but by the settlers who would recant them around the dinner table or read about them in the local paper.

The Nebraska plains that Many Lives called home is where he knew the lay of the land well. No matter how many soldiers were sent after him, they couldn't capture the elusive Many Lives.

US Marshal Harry Finch was now on the way to Omaha in his private train car to meet up with fellow US Marshal Conrad Johnson and to bring down this savage Indian band along with its leader, Many Lives.

It will be good seeing Conrad again, were Harry's thoughts as he sat in his private rail car drinking his second pot of coffee and being rocked to and fro as the train made its way to Omaha. His old train car he had in Washington DC had been signed out to another marshal. This private car was brand new and was furnished with all the latest equipment, including his own telegraph key and it had electric lighting which could be connected wherever there was electric power available.

This was Harry's home away from home and it was equipped with all other luxuries. Leather was his choice for all seating. It had its own outhouse built in and with a window which could be opened for ventilation. Special undercarriage springs made for a more comfortable ride and reduced the noise generated by the metal wheels traveling over the railroad track joints.

Harry had only been involved in the capture of one other Indian, and now, as he sat in his private train car, his thoughts went back to those days on the trail of the elusive Mika.

Mika was a Sioux whose name stood for "raccoon." He was called this because he would paint large, black circles around his eyes for battle, which resembled the eyes of a raccoon. It had taken Harry two months of tracking him before he was captured. Harry had been so close to him on several occasions, but he eluded capture for a long time.

A tradition Harry had picked up from his father was to secure an item from every case he worked on. It was this thought that made him look at the windowed case mounted on the wall of his train car. Inside were items he took from every case that would remind him of that capture.

He spied the long, cylindrical shaft sporting four black crow's feathers attached to one end. At the other was a pointed arrowhead made of flint. This arrow had whizzed past his head and embedded itself in the tree just over his shoulder. Harry now looked at that arrow as a reminder just how close to death he had come at the hand of a savage Indian, and now, he was going after another. Harry also remembered, it was this arrow that lead him to the capture of Mika.

Just as the arrow whizzed past his head, he turned to see the Indian who had delivered it and where he was located. Harry would go to the same spot and look for any clue there he might find to help him track down this Indian who eluded him. Inspecting the area, Harry noticed one of the horse tracks bore shoes. This was something you didn't normally see on an Indian pony. What stood out on this set of horse prints was, there were only three horse shoe prints. One of the shoes was missing.

As often as prints would cross on the trail, he was able to track this one set and capture Mika. Harry considered himself lucky in this capture, although it was good observation that lead to it.

If the stories were true concerning Many Lives, I had best be on my toes one-hundred percent of the time until I capture him, were his thoughts.

To see someone wearing fifty-seven scalps tied around their chest must be something to witness and he tried to visualize what that would look like.

As the train crossed the Nebraska plains, Harry notice several Indians on horseback from time to time, and wondered if any one of them might have been this Indian known as Many Lives.

Looking through his field glasses, he hadn't noticed any of them sporting a large mass of hair in the vicinity of their chest, so he guessed not. He wondered how he would feel and react to someone wanting to take his land and then doing just that, knowing they would kill you and your family to do so.

In good faith they signed a peace treaty, then those who proposed them, broke them. To watch as the settlers in their wagon trains, make sport in seeing how many buffalo they could shoot, or for that matter, how many Indians they could shoot as target practice anytime they would be seen.

I'm afraid I would be doing just what the Indians are doing, Harry thought, looking out the window at the plains as he traveled through it.

There is plenty of land. Harry thought, looking out as far as his eyes could see. It would probably take a person on horseback a good week to cover the land he was seeing. For the first time since joining the US Marshals, Harry questioned how his assignment was going to impact a whole civilization of people.

Many Lives and his band of renegades were just about the last of the Indian hold-outs. They were the few who refused to surrender their weapons and move to a reservation, which was the poorest land the US

Government had set aside for them to live on. The reservation that these Nebraska Indian tribes were being moved into wasn't even in Nebraska, but Florida. A land they weren't even familiar with.

Since the battle of the Little Big Horn and the massacre of General George Armstrong Custer, the government had taken an even more hostile approach with the Indian tribes who refused to move onto the reservations. The victory enjoyed by the Indian that day would be short lived and the last one they would celebrate.

The US Army would increase in numbers. Rounding up all those and moving them onto reservations, those refusing were killed, no questions asked. Small bands of renegade Indians such as the one Many Lives headed up, were tracked down and captured or destroyed.

Many Lives had succeeded in frustrating the whole US Army. They had become weary of the chase, but knew Many Lives needed to be captured. He had been given many opportunities to surrender, his answer was to claim another scalp or two.

Sitting there staring out the window, all these thoughts were being tossed around inside Harry's head. Although his assignment to capture Many Lives was an important one, it wouldn't end the Indian Wars like he thought it would. It would be another twenty years or so and would end with the Battle of Sugar Point in Leech Lake, Minnesota on October 5, 1898.

The war might not end with his capture, but a lot of settler's lives would be spared. The raiding on the settlers had escalated and there were never any survivors to identify those responsible. What was common with all of the settlers who had been killed was there were some Indian arrows found that bore the same likeness, giving proof it was the same band of Indian warriors who conducted the raids.

Harry held two in his hands that had been sent to him when he was given this assignment. The arrows he held, were several inches longer than most Indian arrows. All had three red circles painted around the center, and three long tail feathers that were from the large scavenger birds known as buzzards or vultures. It was a bird common to the western plains. The arrows length along with the long tail feathers would increase the arrows flight and accuracy.

Most settlers were not gunmen, and even though they had rifles and pistols, they probably couldn't hit the broad side of a barn, so the further away the Indian could be when attacking the better.

I wonder why Many Lives and his small band of renegades didn't use rifles. A thought going through Harry's mind, although as deadly as Many Lives was with a bow, he didn't have to use a rifle. *His attacks could be carried out in complete silence if he chose. It would be interesting to hear Conrad's take on this.*

Once again, a smile came across Harry's face at the thought of his friend and associate Conrad, along with his taste buds coming alive remembering the rich flavor of Conrad's coffee. With that thought, Harry headed to the stove and poured himself a cup of coffee which in no way resembled Conrad's.

"I will definitely have Conrad show me how to brew coffee this time," he said out loud, after taking a mouthful of the bitter liquid he had brewed.

Stopping at a couple small towns along the route to Omaha, Harry picked up some needed supplies. One of the items he bought was some already ground coffee beans.

I wonder if Conrad is aware of this new item, Harry questioned in his head. *I wonder what kind of coffee it will make.* Tomorrow, he would know when he arrived in Omaha and reunited with Conrad.

Sometime in the night, Harry was awakened by what he thought were gun shots. He laid in bed and continued listening, but all he heard was the constant ka-thump, ka-thump as steel wheels contacted the joints of the rail. He even got up and stepped outside on the small deck of his rail car, but couldn't make out anything in the darkness nor did he hear any gun shots.

He would check in the morning with the conductor to see if he had heard anything. Until then, he went back inside and once again settled down and it wasn't long before the swaying of the rail car and the constant rumbling had Harry in dreamland once again.

Next morning, Harry made his way to the passenger car and spoke with the conductor who told him there had been some sighting during the night of a small band of Indians who rode close to the train and had drawn some rifle fire from the engineer and brakeman, who fired at them as a warning to stay away. Harry made his way to the locomotive to speak with the engineer and brakeman.

It was confirmed that some Indians were sighted and they had shot a couple of arrows into the cab area which drew rifle fire from the engineer and brakeman. The brakeman handed Harry the arrow that was shot at him. Inspecting the arrow, it was plain to see it was one that came from Many Lives' band of renegades. Its extra length, the three red circles around the middle, and the longer, black tail feathers made it obvious to him, this train was visited by Many Lives last night.

Being given the location of the encounter by the engineer for future use, Harry made his way back to his private car for the remainder of the trip. Around two o'clock that afternoon, they pulled into the train station in Omaha. There on the station's landing was Conrad wearing a big grin in anticipation of his arrival as the train came to a stop.

Harry hadn't told Conrad about him having a private car again, so Conrad wasn't paying any attention to the last car on the train. The train was scheduled for a two-hour layover before continuing its schedule to the east coast and Washington, DC.

Harry stepped from his car just as Conrad looked in Harry's direction. His grin grew upon seeing Harry and he set out in Harry's direction.

"Harry," he said, extending his hand, which Harry took and pulled him into a big old bear hug just as brothers would.

"Good to see ya," they both said together.

Just then, the conductor walked up and they made plans to disconnect Harry's private car which would also be their room for the night, having to wait till tomorrow morning for the next train headed back west, so they could get as close to where Many Lives had attacked the train. Putting Conrad's cases in Harry's private car, they headed to the nearest restaurant and some much needed food.

There would be plenty of time to discuss the assignment later, for now, they needed to catch up on a more personal level.

Chapter 2.

After catching up on their lives over a nice steak, Conrad and Harry headed back to his private car where Harry showed Conrad the can of ground coffee and told him to do his magic.

A short time passed, and then the room was filled with the aroma of brewing coffee.

Harry placed the two arrows he had received in front of Conrad as they sat talking.

"This is what I received that was found at the last settler attack," Harry told him. "From what I've learned, they match others that were found at different attack sites. They also match the one the brake man showed me last night when a small band of Indians galloped alongside our train and shot one of them into the cab of the engine."

"I spoke to several people, while traveling to meet you and also as I waited for you, about this Indian we are going after named Many Lives and his small band of hostile Renegades."

As Conrad spoke, Harry noticed a concern in his tone of voice and questioned him about it.

"Your tone of voice seems troubling," Harry said after listening to Conrad tell what he had heard.

"I am concerned somewhat, Harry. We are going after a band of savages whose leader deems himself invincible, who wears the scalps of many tied to his chest, who doesn't even make use of a rifle or any kind of gun, but bow and arrows only. And, to top that all off, has evaded the whole US Army which had gone after him in numbers."

Judging the coffee to be done, Conrad opened one of the cupboard doors and located two cups which he filled with the steaming, black liquid.

"Fantastic!" Harry told him, as the hot liquid passed over his taste buds. "You will show me how to make coffee while we are together this time."

"You bet, Harry," was all he said.

"I have those same concerns," Harry told him. "We have been given an assignment and it is our job to bring this renegade Indian and his band of killers to justice, and that is what we will do. We need to overlook what rumors we have heard about this Indian known as Many Lives, and approach the assignment like any others. We can't get caught up in worry or questioning our superiors, but just go on about the assignment, get it done, then go on to the next."

"Sounds good, Harry. I guess I just needed to hear all of that from you. After all, I know you well enough that you probably have already put together a plan."

"No, I haven't," Harry confessed. "Only to locate the place where the engineer told me where the train was attacked by who I believe was Many Lives, and see what we might find there that will give me a plan. Other than that, I have nothing."

It was true, I didn't have a plan.

"That doesn't sound like you, Harry," Conrad said. "You usually have a plan all laid out before starting an assignment."

"That's true," Harry stated. "But with the Indian, it seems plans were meant to be broken. I found they never set a pattern to what they did, but lived from day to day, and moment to moment, changing by the minute if need be."

"Well, Harry, from the stories I gathered about this Indian Many Lives, we will need a plan and a darn good one. It sounds eerie to say but this Indian thinks he travels in the spirit world along with his band of renegades, which makes him very dangerous."

Here it was. The reason for Conrad's concern about this assignment. Upon hearing him say the words, I guess I had those same thoughts.

"We both know better than that," Harry finally said. "But it is true. He thinks it's so, and until he is shown otherwise, he will be a lot harder to predict and capture. He will be very dangerous and take chances one would never believe possible, so we will have to stay alert and try to think like him."

Jumping to his feet, Harry yelled out in a high pitched voice, raising both his hands into the air, "I'm invincible!" he yelled out, then again, "I'm invincible!"

Catching on, Conrad rose to his feet and followed suit.

"I'm invincible!" he countered, then together, grasping each other's hands, "we're invincible!"

Harry felt it, and judging by the expression on Conrad's face, he felt it too. It was something one felt, but couldn't put into words. At this instant, outside, a bolt of lightning lit up the heavens in a display so bright it hurt the eyes. Inside the train car, it was as bright as ten noon day suns. This was followed by the far away rumbling of thunder that grew in volume until his rail car shook violently, windows rattled so loud Harry thought they would shatter. Cupboard doors flew open and contents spilled out onto the floor, and his ear drums were ready to explode. Harry let go of Conrad's hands and clasped them over his ears. The short hairs on the back of his neck stood up straight in their familiar warning. All this taking place in a matter of seconds.

And then, suddenly, as quickly as it had taken place, quietness!

What just happened? These words jumped out of Harry's mind. "What just happened?" Harry whispered, unable to speak in a louder tone of voice.

Conrad offered up no explanation, and the silence continued.

"Look Harry!" Conrad's voice cut the silence.

Looking in his direction, Harry's eyes followed Conrad's, amazed at what Harry saw. There on the table were the two arrows Harry had previously shown to Conrad, except now, one was sticking straight up with its point buried deep in the tabletop, the other was lying next to it, broken in half.

"What the…?" Conrad started to say, but Harry held up his hand in Conrad's face to stop him.

Rather than speak, Harry tilted his head towards the door and Conrad followed him outside.

Once outside, they both stood there in silence.

"Look!" sounded Conrad's voice once again breaking the silence.

All around us, people were looking up into the night's sky. No one speaking, but all with the same bewildering look on their faces as they strained their faces to the heavens, looking for some sort of explanation as to what just took place.

They had seen and heard what we had just seen and heard, Harry's thoughts told him.

"They saw and heard it too Harry," Conrad finally spoke. "What do you make of that?"

"I don't know," he told him. "Something very, very special happened here for our benefit I believe. Maybe, we shouldn't put question to it, but, like a few moments ago, simply raise our hands once again and stand in awe."

"How are we going to test it?" Conrad whispered.

"Test what?" Harry replied back, not sure what he was getting at.

"You know," he whispered. "Invincible! Are we invincible?"

"Are you out of your mind?" Harry asked. "You don't believe what I think you just referred to. Do you?"

"The Indians believe in the supernatural, so why shouldn't we?" he questioned. "After all, look around at all these people. They heard and saw the same thing we did. We didn't make what happened up! It was real."

"You're right," Harry agreed. "But what happened didn't in any way affect us as a human being."

Doubling up his fist, Harry punched Conrad in the stomach. His response was to double over and say loudly, "ummmmphs!"

"There," Harry said. "You felt that, correct?"

"Sure I did, Harry, but that doesn't mean anything," he told Harry. "Being invincible you can still feel pain, it's just that you can't be killed."

"Okay," Harry finally said. "Enough of this talk about being invincible."

Turning to head back inside his rail car, Harry was stopped dead in his tracks. There, sticking out from the door was a long arrow with black feathers and three red rings painted around its center.

Conrad must have seen it at the same instant Harry had.

"What in the hell is that?" his voice taking on a low grumble.

Harry walked up to the arrow, standing eye level with the three red rings, but not daring to touch it yet.

A quick glance over his shoulder at Conrad told Harry he was thinking the same as Harry. *Was this arrow real?*

Looking back to the arrow, Harry slowly reached up to touch it. It was a real arrow alright. Harry grasped it firmly in his hand and gave it a solid outward pull and it came loose from the door.

Harry opened the door. Turning back toward Conrad, Harry indicated to go inside.

Without hesitation, Conrad picked up items from the floor and put on a pot of coffee. Harry laid the arrow on the table top next to the broken in half one.

Picking up the two pieces, Harry placed them next to the one on the table. They were identical.

"Explain that, Harry!" said Conrad, looking at the two.

Harry pulled the other arrow out of the tabletop and placed it next to the two. All three were identical. Seeing this, the short hairs on his neck once again stood up. But this time it felt different. Gone was the feeling of being watched, instead it was one of caution, and with it came a calmness to his wellbeing he hadn't witnessed or felt before.

"What is it Harry? What's happening now?" Conrad's voice echoed somewhere in the canyons of his mind.

So distant was his voice, Harry turned to face Conrad to make sure he was still standing next to Harry. Along with Conrad's far away voice was another voice. This one sounding like a lone coyote in the middle of the night, sounding way off in the distance and he was howling, "follow the signs, Harry. Follow the signs."

And just as quickly as the lightning and thunder clasp had come, it was gone, and with it the howling coyote's voice.

"Harry! Speak to me, Harry." Conrad's voice Harry could hear loud and clear, seemly waking him from some sort of trance Harry was temporarily under.

"Follow the signs," Harry whispered, coming out of his dreamlike state.

"Follow the signs," repeated Conrad. "What signs are you talking about, Harry?" he questioned.

"I'm not sure," Harry whispered back. "It was a voice I heard a moment ago that spoke to my subconscious. That's what it was saying to me, 'follow the signs.'"

"This is all spooky to me, Harry," Conrad said. "Guess we will have to wait and see what it all means," he concluded. "Want a coffee?"

A slight knock was heard on the door.

Harry opened it to find the railway station manager standing there.

"Just wanted to confirm the train will be pulling into the station right at nine o'clock in the morning. It's scheduled to take on water, passengers, and pick up you and your car, this shouldn't take more than a half hour."

"We are scheduled to stop in Dusty Hollow where my car will be disconnected, is that correct?" Harry asked, wanting to be sure.

"Yes. You're good to go Mr. Finch," he said then added. "That coffee sure smells delightful."

"It is," Harry told him. "Would you like a cup?"

Harry had found over the course of time, whenever the opportunity presented itself to make a new friend, to do so. That way, you have someone you can get to verify who you are if need be in the future, and someone else you can put at ease, so that you could ask questions and get a straight answer and not make them feel like they are being questioned. The train station manager was Nate

Parker and he knew everyone in town, or so it seemed and was probably known by many as the town's gossip.

Sitting down with a coffee in front of him, he saw the arrows and picking up one remarked, "Looks like one of Many Lives," then looking at it a little more closely corrected himself, "I believe it is one of Many Lives."

Looking at Conrad, Harry slid into the seat and began to question Nate.

"You know about this Indian called Many Lives?" Harry asked. "How do you know about him and more so, the relationship to the arrow you hold in your hand?"

"Everyone knows about Many Lives," he told Harry. "You don't see many of his arrows unless he wants to be known for an attack, then, he will leave one or two as a signature. Yup. Same feathers, three red rings, and the extra length. This is one of his."

Harry was about to ask Nate, where did he get his information, but Nate beat Harry to the question.

"Randy Eastman," a name he blurted out. "Owner of the Omaha Star Gazette. He is also an Indian historian. There isn't much he doesn't know where the Indian is concerned," he continued.

"Will you introduce us to him?" Harry asked. "I wanted to ask him many questions, especially about Many Lives."

"Sure," he said, draining his coffee cup. "He'll still be at the paper."

All three of them finished their coffee together, then left Harry's car and followed Nate to the Omaha Star Gazette's office where he introduced Conrad and Harry to Randy.

They shook hands, then Nate said he had to get back to the station.

"So! The US Army couldn't capture Many Lives so they sent for two US Marshals to do the job," Randy said. It wasn't a question, but more a statement. "Well, good luck."

"Two US Marshals are an Army in itself," Harry told him. "Now, if we were Texas Rangers!" This statement drew a smile from him, and from Conrad and Harry.

"Well, you will wish you were two Texas Rangers, if you plan on going after and capturing Many Lives."

Face to face with a serious tone to his voice, he asked, "You do know who this Indian Many Lives is, along with the ones who ride with him, don't you?"

"Only what I have heard," Harry answered. "I'm hoping you can add to my knowledge."

"Where did you get that arrow?" he asked, indicating to the one Harry held in his hand.

"Believe it or not, I found it sticking in the rear door of my private rail car." Harry told him, holding it up so he could see it more closely. "Is it one of Many Lives?"

As his hand touched the arrow Harry held out to him, a small bolt of lightning passed between them, causing them both to jump back. Releasing the arrow, it fell to the floor, where right before their eyes it turned into ashes.

Three bewildered faces looked down on the pile of ashes on the floor where the arrow had just landed.

"Holy smoke!" exclaimed Conrad, mystified, like Harry and Randy were.

"Holy smokes isn't the word for it," Harry said, after a few moments spent to get his thoughts together.

"You need to leave here right this instant," Randy said, his voice suddenly filled with horror.

"Get out!" he yelled, pushing them both out the door. "I'll see you later in your rail car. Till then, be very careful and say nothing to no one about what you witnessed here just now."

They returned to Harry's rail car without incident. Once inside, Harry locked the doors, pulled down window shades, and instructed Conrad to put on coffee.

Conrad and Harry were both seated with their hands wrapped around hot coffee cups, staring at the two remaining arrows when, off in the distant night sky, they heard the far away rumble of an approaching thunder storm.

Looking over at Conrad, Harry felt the short hairs on the back of his neck start to jump.

Chapter 3

Many Lives and his renegade braves sat around the campfire. The raid that day had brought success and the addition of two more scalps to decorate the cross the chest gun belt Many Lives wore.

Running his hands over them, he gently patted them. These two, he would treasure above all as they were as white as freshly fallen snow.

At one time, they were streaked with red, and Many Lives thought about leaving them like that, but riding through a heavy rainfall they were washed clean and now Many Lives kept them snowy white.

The Bakers were still living out of their wagon, having not made up their minds where they would build their small plains home when Many Lives and his braves attacked. It was a short lived raid as the older Bakers were no match for a bunch of Indians set on killing and scalping. Old man Baker was killed almost from the start. One of Many Lives arrows buried deep in the center of his chest, where it had pierced his age old heart.

Mrs. Baker wasn't so lucky. She was captured and forced to undergo several hours of rape by the young renegades before Many Lives himself drove his long knife into her heart after listening to her shrieks of pain, as he cut the scalp from her head.

Over twenty soldiers had trailed Many Lives and his braves, losing them in the rocky landscape as they headed into the nearby area known as Red Rocks of the Plains by both Indian and soldier.

Red Rocks was a vast area where anyone could disappear and not be found. Here in this vast rock formation, Many Lives and his band of renegades made their home. Many a soldier who had entered on the trail of Many Lives never came out and their bodies were never found.

There were stories told of great thunder and lightning storms over this area where it would be sunny and clear in the surrounding areas. Travelers on trains passing this area at night told stories of a bluish, green glow in the sky that lite up the whole area.

Many believed Many Lives was a ghost and Red Rocks is where he lived. Part of this mystique fueled the flames of special spiritual powers that Many Lives seemed to have along with his band of savages. Other than the one where he couldn't be killed, Many Lives surrounded himself in this folk lore and mystique generated about him and he would play into it.

Of course, these stories seemed to grow in stature the more times they were told.

That little bolt of lightning soon became a thunderest one that shook the ground and felled great trees, and anyone near it when it struck would be burned to ashes.

Many Lives stood in wonder as to what sign it was trying to relay to him.

Among the soldiers, if they were trailing Many Lives and his tracks entered Red Rocks they were to abandon the chase. Regardless if one believed or not, just the fact Many Lives and his warriors were still free and alive and had evaded capture by the whole US Army just added to the overall aura surrounding Many Lives and his band of savages.

Many Lives was a very smart Indian and he grew up learning to hunt, track, and to make himself invisible to the animal he was seeking. He learned to cover his scent using whatever was at hand. He could camouflage himself so well you could just about walk over him without seeing him.

As he grew, he became more efficient at this. When he became a warrior, he learned how important these skills had been and used them to create this mystique generated about him by the white man and soldiers. Even as a young warrior, he indulged in what the Indian referred to as counting coup. This awarded one great prestige amongst his peers.

To count coup one must always put himself in danger of being wounded or killed by his enemy, be it another warrior or a white man or soldier. It simply meant the touching of another, be it by bow, couping stick or by the hand, this being the greatest of the three and awarding the greatest prestige in the tribe. Coup could also be counted for other acts such as, the taking of an enemy's horse from its place outside of his teepee or dwelling place or his weapon.

Different tribes had different ways of showing those who had counted coup. Some tribes painted designs on a special piece of clothing. Others, special bars such as the soldiers wore to define their rank. And others, such was the case in Many Lives tribe, the eagle feather.

For each coup, one was awarded an eagle feather but only if he counted that coup without injury. If he was wounded in the process, he was still awarded the eagle feather but he had to stain it red. These eagle feathers were often attached to their spear or their couping stick, which they used in the process of counting coup. Some wore them braided into their hair.

Many Lives chose to display his in the form of a blanket he draped over his horse's neck which also gave the appearance at quick glance that the horse had wings. It was easy to see where the story came from that he rode on a flying horse.

What made Many Lives the ruthless warrior that he is, was because he truly believed he was a spiritual being. His horse blanket of many eagle feathers contested to the fact he was a great warrior. The feathers that were stained red indicating he was wounded in battle; he wore breaded into his hair. These he wore proudly, an indication he had survived the white man's attempt to kill him and a sign they had not succeeded.

Not only was Many Lives known by the white man and soldiers, he was also recognized among his own people. Enemy warriors feared him, where others held him up in great esteem, being honored if they could ever help him in any way.

When Many Lives would enter a village, he was always given the seat next to the chief. A game the youngsters would play whenever he was in their village was to see if they could count coup with him or his warriors. This was a game enjoyed by all. It was fun to watch a young brave try to sneak up close enough where he could run up and touch him. Many Lives always had a few eagle feathers he would reward them with if they succeeded.

Many Lives would tell the story about the time he had counted coup on the greatest warrior of them all, Geronimo.

Just the mention of this warrior's name conjured up visions of greatness and awe amongst the Indian villages. A figure of white man's defiance and Many Lives wanted that same recognition.

As the white settlers moved into the Great Plains, they were met by the Indian warriors and conflicts developed. The US Government sent in its army of soldiers to quell the Indians. Once they were proven to be liars and to break their own treaties with the Indian, the Indian rebelled even greater and gave birth to the warrior chiefs such as Geronimo, Crazy Horse, and Sitting Bull who fought the army soldiers at every turn.

Many Lives strove to be one of those great warrior chiefs. His journey started quite by accident. He was hunting with his brother Twisted Knee and several others when they came upon two wagons of settlers which were being escorted across the plains by ten army soldiers. Knowing his longer arrows could be fired from a greater distance, he and his hunting friends hid amongst the rocks that were several hundred yards away from the wagons and army soldiers.

Staying hidden, Many Lives instructed these braves to fire their arrows up into the air so they would rain down on the unsuspecting wagons and soldiers. To those in the wagons and to the soldiers, these arrows appeared to fall from the sky. Several soldiers were wounded that day, also several arrows were collected so the soldiers could recognize what tribe they came from.

The length wasn't recognized, but the arrow's head pointed to Apache. Several of the Indian scouts, fired these longer arrows and were astonished at the distance they could be fired from and still be accurate. It wouldn't be until the first settlers were killed that Many Lives would be acknowledged as the Indian responsible.

Many Lives would be captured and wounded three times. With each capture, he escaped. After the third, he vowed never to be captured again. With his brother

Twisted Knee and his best friend Smiling Face, he went on to form a small band of nine warriors.

Each warrior had to have counted at least ten coups to be added to his band of warriors. Although 'warriors' was a name he liked his band to be called, they would go on to be called, savages, marauders, and renegades.

Ten, for some reason, had a meaning to him and wherever he could use that number he did, such as ten arrows in his quiver. Every ten days he would demand they be in Red Rocks, where they would feast on the spoils of battles fought during that time. They would chant, dance, eat, make new weapons, and if they had captured a woman, she was used at this time before she was killed. It was Many Lives' knife who ended the lives of these women.

In the beginning, there had been only one woman to have escaped the final ending to their celebration and several days after escaping she hung herself, tormented by what she had gone through.

She would be the first and only one to ever escape.

Women were used and then killed at the place of battle and not brought back to their camp at Red Rocks. Red Rocks being Many Lives' home, he knew every inch of it. Every nook and cranny. Every hiding place. Every animal that made its home there.

He and his warriors had traps set all over Red Rocks. They had supplies stored in many different places. Extra weapons had been made and hid for emergencies. There were a number of caves that had entrances so well disguised, you could literally be standing right in front of it and not see it.

Soldiers following Many Lives into Red Rocks were confronted by what they didn't find, so the tale that he could vanish grew. Later, when soldiers would enter Red Rocks and were killed, their bodies were hidden in one of these caves so they were never found, thus fueling the mystique around Many Lives and his renegade warriors.

Many Lives basked in his notoriety for he had heard all that was said about him and his warriors. He couldn't believe how easy it was to fool the army soldiers into believing he possessed some kind of supernatural powers, although he believed himself to be invincible and no white man's bullet or weapon could kill him.

It was a lack of training on the soldiers' part that led Many Lives to be so successful in his attacks on their companies, but it was also his ability to rain down arrows from a greater distance that gave him the advantage.

The vigorous training that all of his braves underwent was superior to that of the white soldier. Games of war were always being played when not in a real battle which was rare, because Many Lives went looking for settlers to attack. He wanted nothing more than to raid the white settlers and add to his ever growing number of scalps and to increase the stories that each raid generated throughout the land.

Many Lives had recently started watching the Iron Horse as it crossed the Plains. Sparks from the locomotives sometimes would set the prairie grasses on fire and if it wasn't for Many Lives being there to put them out, much land would be destroyed. He would do anything he could think of to stop the Iron Horse from crossing the plains, which he considered his people's land.

His braves would remove some of the rail spikes so when the Iron Horse passed over those sections of track with spikes removed, the tracks would come apart and the Iron Horse would crash. Depending on if the train was carrying passengers or not would determine his next move. Just the crash itself took many lives and stopped the influx of settlers who were entering the plains area by train.

Many Lives decided not to attack the Iron Horse, but to just rain down some arrows at any movement he saw. This left many arrows that could be used to identify him and his small band of renegades.

The night Finch and his special train car passed through the plains, Many Lives and his band of renegades were headed to their home at Red Rocks, this being the start of his rest after raiding for ten days, so he had fired only one arrow at the end car as it passed by.

Many Lives then headed to Red Rocks with his band of warriors not knowing what would take place in Omaha later, concerning that one arrow.

Chapter 4

Harry and Conrad were glad when the train pulled into Dusty Hollow and his car was unhitched, both ready to get this assignment under way.

Harry wondered whatever happened to Randy, the owner of the newspaper and Indian historian, who was going to get together with them but hadn't shown up after he basically threw them from his office. Harry couldn't get the look on his face out of his mind. *He was definitely frightened about what had taken place,* he thought.

Trying to think why Randy hadn't shown wasn't what was going to be needed for them to bring in the elusive Many Lives and his band of renegades, so more thinking why Randy hadn't kept their meeting was now wasting precious time.

The day was already hot and sticky as they made their way to the livery stable where horses were saddled and waiting for them.

"Saddle them up as soon as I heard the train arrive," they were told. "Fuller, the owner of the stable said he would catch up with you, when you returned to settle up. He needed to bring some supplies out to the Jenkins place. Besides, you're US Marshals, and we can trust ya," this said with a slight smirk on his face.

IF we return! Conrad's thoughts told him before he could stop them.

As a US Marshal, you couldn't let any signs or thoughts of doubt creep into your sub-conscience before or during an assignment, especially an assignment where you could be killed at any time. You needed to keep your mind alert and focused on the job at hand, aware of your surroundings, of what could be around the next bend that could possibly kill you or cause you great harm.

There was no room for negative thoughts, if you expected to come out alive and unscathed in your pursuit of the bad guy. Never mind a savage Indian who was convinced no white man's bullets or weapons could harm him and he was the leader of a band of renegades who thought the same thing.

I need to shake these thoughts, Conrad thought to himself. *These thoughts could put both Harry and me in added danger.*

Just hearing some of the stories where Many Lives was concerned, conjured up visions of the spirit world and those that were Many Lives' protectors. Conrad knew the Indians had many gods they bowed down to and danced for, so they could reap all the rewards that were marked for them. They had a god for everything.

Could there be substance to the stories he had heard? Conrad didn't see why not.

Just because I don't believe the things the Indian believes, doesn't mean they can't be true. The thought snuck in before he could stop it and he knew he would need to talk to Harry and get his advice, if he was to not think of the spiritual aspects he had already witnessed in this assignment.

"Can you point us in the direction of Dry Creek?" Conrad heard Harry ask.

"Sure can," the livery boy told him, and gave him directions.

It was almost a day's ride to the area where the engineer had told him he had seen the small band of Indians who attacked the train, and whose arrow he showed him, which he believed to be one of Many Lives.

The area known as Dry Creek was just that. Here was a dried up creek bed that followed the railroad tracks.

"It'll be getting dark soon," Harry said. "We probably should find a place to make camp for the night, besides I need a cup of coffee."

"I'm with you Harry," Conrad said. "Besides, my backside has had enough saddle time for the day."

Harry nodded his head in agreement.

Off to their left about one-hundred yards away was a large rock formation and Harry headed for it.

As it turned out, several others had made camp there in the past.

There was a fire pit lined with small rocks and even several dry tree limbs.

Getting a fire started, Conrad brought out the coffee pot and the can of ground coffee Harry had given him earlier. They had brought several canteens of water with them, not knowing what the water situation would be, so there was plenty to make a large pot of coffee.

As the coffee boiled, Harry went walking around to see if he could spot anything of value to them. Finding a few small pieces of wood and nothing else, Harry returned to the campsite.

"I could smell that coffee from a couple hundred feet away," Harry told Conrad. "Is it about ready?"

"It is, Harry!" Conrad told him. "Piping hot and black. Just the way you like it."

Bringing the steaming cup close to his nose, Harry took a big sniff of the coffee filled steam rising from it. A mini-sip brought a smile to Harry's face as his taste buds came alive and the rich flavor attacked his sensors.

"My, oh my, is that good," Harry told him. "Don't know which I like better, brewed over a stove or boiled over the open campfire?"

"Two differences in taste, Harry. I like the taste of the campfires smoke mixed in."

"Me too," Harry replied, smiling.

When nighttime falls on the prairie, unless there is a full moon, it gets dark quickly.

"Harry," Conrad's voice cut into the quietness of the darkened sky.

The only other sounds to be heard was the crackling sounds from the fire, and a low humming sound coming from Harry.

"Ya, Conrad," Harry answered, really wanting to just sit in the quietness of the early night and enjoy his cup of coffee.

"Do you believe in the spirit world Harry?" Conrad asked after sitting for a few minutes.

"If you mean do I believe there is a God and a Heaven, yes I do," Harry answered.

"That's not what I mean, Harry," his voice in a whisper. "I mean a spirit world like the Indians believe in?"

"To a certain degree, I do, but I don't believe such things like this Many Lives possessing some extraordinary powers which would keep him from being killed, or make him invisible. Is that what you mean?" Harry asked.

"How would you explain the things we have seen the last couple of days then, Harry?" Conrad asked.

Harry picked up Conrad's concern by the tone of his voice and knew he was struggling with this assignment. They would be going into Many Lives land, his home, a place where no one who had entered ever returned. Those were the facts, the reality that you might not live, that this might be the end of your life. The feeling wasn't new. It's a feeling you get at the beginning of every assignment. It goes with the job.

"One thing I've learned over the years, there are happenings that go on around us that we can't explain and no matter how hard we try to reason it all out we can't. Take the hairs on my neck. I don't understand why they act the way they do to alert me to danger, but I accept them and have learned to channel their meanings."

The expression on Conrad's face told Harry he was trying to grasp the words Harry was saying.

"What we witnessed with the storm, the arrows and my hearing a voice, did that all come from some spirit world or place? I don't know," Harry continued. "But I do know, no one is immune to an ounce of lead. Many Lives and the braves who travel with him have been extremely lucky. He has surrounded himself with this story of protection from the spirit world and people believe it. But there are answers to everything."

The coffee pot was almost empty so he offered it to Conrad.

"Go ahead, Harry. I'll make some more in a bit."

Pouring the last of the coffee, Harry continued.

"The stories that tell of Many Lives not being able to be killed by no white man's bullet stems from his surviving the Battle of the Little Big Horn. Now as I recall there were over two thousand Indians there that day up against a few hundred soldiers. A small amount of Indians was killed while over two hundred and fifty soldiers were lost. How much of the battle did Many Lives see?" Harry asked. "No one knows! My guess would be very little."

Seeing Conrad perk up some in listening to what Harry was offering as a reason why things appear the way they have been, he continued with his explanation.

"There were very few Indians lost in that battle. Does that make every Indian that survived invincible to the white man's bullets? Of course not, unless you wanted to start a story about yourself that would be like a superstition. You see, Conrad, there are answers out there. As we uncover the facts that go along with the story, you will see that Many Lives is no one special, has no supernatural powers. If you shoot him, he will die. This you can believe as real."

Harry was about to change the subject when off in the distance they both heard him. A lone voice calling out into the night.

AWOOOOOOOOOOOOOOO! AWOOO, AWOOO, AWOOOOOOOOOOOOOOO!

As the coyote spoke, it brought back Harry's memory of the one he had heard that told him to read the signs.

"He sounds lonely," Conrad said. They both listened to see if he would receive an answer. No answer came.

After a couple more calls, the night became quiet again. The only sounds being the crackling of the fire which was burning down and whose glowing ashes created a comforting feeling.

"Tired, Harry?" Conrad asked.

"I am," Harry replied.

As Conrad spoke, he was also unrolling his blanket, which he placed several feet from the fire.

"I know you came out to visit when Molly passed, then again when I received my promotion but I just want to say thank you again, Harry."

"Well, you worked hard for the promotion and there isn't anyone that deserved it more then you," Harry told him. "I'm mighty proud of you and happy to have you as my partner once again."

"Same here, Harry."

"You said you're tired. I'll take the first watch," Harry told him. "From here on out, we'll have to be on guard so let's do the usual."

"Two on. Two off. You got it Harry."

"Go to sleep, now. You know how quickly these first two hours go by?" Harry reminded him.

"Want me to put on a pot of coffee before I turn in, Harry?"

"No," Harry answered. "But plan on putting one on just before your shift ends, okay."

"Okay, Harry. See you in two hours."

This was Harry's first night out under the stars in sometime, and it felt good. He always liked the outdoors. Deep inside, Harry longed for Amanda.

Soon, Conrad's snoring sounds were added to the crackling fire.

It had been a long day with many questions, some answered and some not answered. But Harry was pretty confident that over the next few days, more would be revealed about Many Lives, and Conrad and Harry would be able to locate him and his band of renegades. What Harry didn't know was, were they going to be able to take him in alive. Harry hoped they could but he also had his doubts.

Many Lives had murdered many settlers as well as army soldiers, so he must figure his life would end with a white man's rope in a hanging, plus he had sworn never to be taken in alive.

Harry's goal in every case was to bring the subject in alive, but that depended on the subject. In his attempt to put Conrad to ease, voicing out loud his thoughts also helped Harry, too. Harry wished he could have answers for all Conrad's questions, but Harry didn't. Some answers they would just have to find out as they went.

Harry had been in contact with both commanders at Fort Kearney and Fort Omaha and both had pledged their support and told him that Harry had only to ask and they would have a regiment of soldiers at their disposal. And sitting here listening to the crackling of the fire along with Conrad's snoring, Harry knew they would probably have to call on them. He might have been a little hasty in thinking Conrad and Harry could do a job that armies hadn't been able to do, but time would tell.

Two hours went by quickly, and soon it was time to wake Conrad and Harry get some shut eye himself.

I didn't think I was that tired, but I can honestly say, I don't remember my head hitting the saddle.

Harry's dreams this night would take him deep into Red Rocks and the home of Many Lives as he searched every inch of the place. Where Conrad was he didn't know. There were signs galore that told Harry Many Lives had been here, but had left before Harry arrived. It seemed Harry was always two steps behind him. And where in tar nation was Conrad. Harry searched for Conrad but couldn't locate him.

Where there had been no tracks previously, Harry now saw a number of horse tracks, all unshod. The

Indian never shod their horses which made it harder to track. You never knew if the tracks you followed were Indian ponies or wild horses.

In this case, Harry figured them to be Many Live and his braves.

Having made a big circle around Red Rocks, Harry knew these tracks were made in the last three hours. This was the closest Harry had been to Many Lives since Conrad and Harry had started on this assignment.

Out of the corner of his eye, Harry caught some movement, nothing much, just a single sliver of something, then all movement stopped, frozen in an instant. Then time resumed but now in slow motion.

The movement Harry saw was now clear. It was an Indian arrow and it was headed right at him. He watched in awe as it got closer and closer to him. Harry felt no immediate danger from it.

It came closer, so close now he could count the three red rings around its center. Harry could make out the black vulture feathers on the back of the long shaft which he could look down and follow its path backward to where it had been released.

The distance between them was great, but the face seemed to be only a few feet away.

There was no doubt in Harry's mind about the face he was looking at, Harry was face to face with Many Lives, himself.

In his hair were many eagle feathers stained red. The face covered in colorful war paint. His chest was covered with the many scalps he had taken from his victims. Dropping his eyes lower, Harry saw the horse blanket of more eagle feathers arranged around the horse's neck, so they actually looked to be wings on his horse.

Harry's eyes re-focused back on the shaft which was now about to enter his chest. As he watched it inch closer and closer, a calm came over Harry like he had never felt before. He would have thought that he would be on the brink of hysteria seeing Many Lives face to face and eyeing the arrow which was now only a few feet away, but he wasn't. Just as the arrow was about to pierce his chest, Harry reached up and grabbed it with his right hand stopping its forward motion and saving his life.

Harry looked at the shaft in wonder. In his hand, he held an arrow which was meant to kill him which only seconds earlier was traveling at Harry with that intent, and now he held it in the palm of his hand. Opening his hand, Harry saw and counted the three red circles on the shaft which was one of Many Lives trademarks. There on the back were the vulture feathers, another one of Many Lives markings.

Harry's eyes slowly lifted up from the shaft and once again focused on the face of Many Lives. This time, the face had a grin on it. Seeing his face with that grin made Harry want to return it, which he did. Here they were, two warriors facing each other for the first time, and both wearing a grin on their faces.

Harry wanted to lift his rifle from its case but was unable to. Instead, he raised his hand in what would have been a way of greeting, but now it was done as a form of recognition for the hand Harry held up held Many Lives' arrow.

Harry watched as Many Lives raised his hand, open palm out. Once it was fully extended, he slowly curled it into a fist. His sign meaning there would be another time where they would meet again. Harry slowly raised his other hand, grasping the arrow in them both, snapped it in half and tossed the two pieces to the ground.

It seemed like a long time that they just sat there looking at each other before Many Lives reined his pony and disappeared from sight, leaving Harry alone in the quietness.

Then the quietness was shattered by Conrad's voice, yelling, "Harry, Harry, wake up. You're having a bad dream!"

Chapter 5

"Harry, Harry, wake up!" Conrad repeated. This time grabbing Harry by the shoulders and shaking him awake.

Abruptly opening his eyes, Harry jerked his body from its prone position to one of sitting upright.

The grogginess of sleep was replaced instantly by one of wide awakeners.

At that same moment, Harry felt the short hairs rise up on the back of his neck screaming out their warning. A quick glance around and Harry caught some movement. Instantly he recognized it, and without warning to Conrad, violently reached up and grabbing his shirt front and pulled him over and out of the path of an incoming arrow. Rolling over with him, and out of instinct, Harry drew his pistol and placed several rounds in the direction he had seen the movement.

Conrad, now fully recovered from Harry's sudden outburst and the loud boom, boom, boom of his pistol next to Conrad's head, had his weapon in hand and looking in the same direction Harry's was. After a few minutes, Harry stood up ignoring Conrad's objections.

"He's gone," Harry told him. Knowing that it was probably Many Lives himself who was there.

"How can you be so sure?" Conrad asked, as he stood keeping his pistol in hand and glancing around.

"If that's fresh coffee in that pot, pour me a cup and I'll tell ya."

A pot of coffee later and having recanted his dream to Conrad, Harry knew that as far as either one of them getting anymore sleep that probably wasn't going to happen, so the remainder of the night was spent in catching up on their private lives.

There was a bond they both felt growing between them and both felt a stronger need to protect the others back. First light found both Harry and Conrad looking over the area where Harry had seen the movement and in the direction he had delivered several rounds from his pistol. They were just about to give up finding anything and head back to break up camp and continue onto Red Rocks when Harry spied it. There on the ground was a couple minute spots of what he believed to be blood.

The dry earth had almost completely absorbed them, but hadn't.

"Look here," Harry said, pointing in the direction he saw the blood.

"Is that blood, Harry?" an excited Conrad asked, now kneeling down next to Harry.

"I think so," he answered. "And look! Doesn't that appear to be a footprint?"

"It sure looks like one," Conrad agreed. "I think we need to keep looking around. Maybe we need to go out a few hundred yards and see if there are any more signs."

It was easy to pick up the excitement in Conrad's voice thought Harry. *Heck, I'm excited, too.*

"Over here, Harry," Conrad's voice echoed. "Over here."

Looking at the ground as Harry made his way to where Conrad stood, a flash from last night's dream entered his mind. What Harry hadn't noticed was when Many Lives raised his hand there was blood running down his arm which dripped onto the ground.

Stopping dead in his tracks, Harry's mind tried to comprehend this new fact and what its meaning was. Looking at the ground where Conrad was pointing were more small drops of what appeared to be blood.

"What's that smell?" Harry asked, raising his head and sniffing the air. "Smells like horse manure."

Conrad, putting his nose to the air, smelled it also and walking around came upon a pile of it.

"Over here," he called out again, standing next to the pile of horse crap.

"Judging by the many horse prints, I'd say he was here for some time. Wouldn't you agree, Harry?"

"I would, but I don't understand it. Why wouldn't he have erased all prints and signs that he was here? And why wouldn't he have buried the horse manure? Doesn't make any sense to me," Harry told Conrad, picking up a small twig and poking the pile of crap. It had been there for a while.

"If he was hurt, maybe he couldn't," Harry told him. Thinking again of the shots I had taken at him.

"It's almost like some kind of sign. Whaaaaa."

Before Conrad could get another word out, Harry's voice, now filled with Conrad's excitement, blurted out,

"Follow the signs! This is what the meaning to the other voice Harry heard, the coyote's voice telling me to follow the signs."

"Okay. Okay, Harry! Let's go back and sit down and you can re-tell your dream. Maybe there will be something more that you overlooked the first time, but now with the knowledge you are searching for more signs, well, maybe you will see more."

Something Harry remembered when they returned to camp was neither one of them had bothered to see if they could find the arrow that Harry had pulled Conrad from out of its path.

Now, looking around they found it lying on the ground, broken in half, having hit a rock.

The thought of Harry in the dream of breaking the arrow in half and tossing it to the ground had a new meaning. Another sign, to speak of.

"What's the meaning behind the broken arrow, Harry?" Conrad asked.

"If I recall, the broken arrow is the Indians peace symbol," Harry told him. "Not exactly sure what it means here though."

"Well, Harry. Could that be Many Lives' way of saying he wants peace between you two?"

"That's an interesting concept, I must say, Conrad. And one to ponder on for a while."

Harry had to admit it was an interesting observation.

If Many Lives was in fact offering up a peace between them, he had reached out twice now. And me, breaking the arrow I had caught and tossing it on the ground between us, he summed up that peace is what I wanted also, and that is why he rode away. Content there was peace between us.

Harry shared his thoughts with Conrad, who suggested they return to Dusty Hollow, wire Randy and tell him of this new happening and see what his thoughts were.

"We need some answers Harry and I think Randy can supply them," was what Conrad said. "He can tell us, and if he can't let's wire the commander at one of the forts for his advice."

Plans were made to leave in the morning and return to Dusty Hollow and telegraph Randy and wire the commanders of both forts.

"Someone will have some answers for us, Harry," said Conrad. "I'm sure of it."

As night replaced the day, the lone coyote was once again attempting to find a mate.

Awoooooooooooo, Awooo, Awooo, Awoooooooooo! He sang into the night. Still, he received no answer.

The night was uneventful and passed quickly. Conrad had last watch so there was hot coffee when Harry woke. Breaking up camp, they made their way back to Dusty Hollow, neither one aware of the many eyes that followed them.

Back in Dusty Hollow, Harry hitched up to the telegraph line and sent his messages over to both forts. He received a telegraph back from a Corporal Ellis at Fort Omaha advising Harry that Colonel Benjamin Pratte with twenty soldiers was on the way to Dusty Hollow, headed to Red Rocks and should arrive tomorrow around noon.

Harry then sent a wire to the telegraph office with a message for Randy at the Omaha Star Gazette. A message back informed him that Randy had left town, suddenly.

The aroma of boiling coffee once again invaded Harry's sensors and he watched as Conrad took two cups from the cupboard and placed them on the table next to the arrows still there. Gone was the one that had been rendered to ashes.

"What's on your mind, Harry?" asked Conrad, pouring the two cups full with the steaming, black liquid causing Harry's taste buds to jump around in his mouth.

"I was wondering why Randy left town," Harry told him between sips.

"Was there anything said in the telegram? Doesn't it seem strange for him to just up and leave?"

"I guess without being able to ask him we will never know," Harry said.

"Well, let's hope that Colonel Pratte can supply us with some answers tomorrow," said Conrad, draining his cup and pouring a refill.

"We can speculate all we want and drive ourselves nuts, so let's just wait until tomorrow and hopefully the Colonel will have all our answers or at least be able to shed some light on the subject." Even as Harry voiced this, he had an uncomfortable feeling.

Dreams that night was centered on the soldiers and Indians in battle. Harry was an eagle flying around over the battlefield and observed Many Lives separating his band of renegade warriors to engage the soldiers.

Harry watched from above as the two bands of Indians set deadly traps for the soldiers. He wished there were some way to warn the soldiers of impending danger, but for some reason Harry couldn't go low enough for them to see him. Besides, he was an eagle.

Harry circled and watched as the Indians engaged the soldiers in such a way, they split ranks and once they did that, they were at the mercy of Many Lives arrows as they fired them from some distance away and rained them down on the soldiers.

Harry watched firsthand the effect the longer arrows had in this kind of battle. Hidden by the rocks they were protected from the soldier's rifle fire, all the time moving in such a way as to lure the soldiers into their trap. All Harry could do was to watch from above. He circled above looking down on what would soon be a total massacre of the soldiers. As Harry circled overhead, he wondered where Conrad was. Harry looked around and didn't see him anywhere.

Sighting a large rock formation, Harry circled above in hopes of being able to land on top of it. If he could land on top of it, Harry would still have an eagle eye view of the battle which was taking place below. From this point, it was easy to see the formation of the soldiers which had split up into two small groups and moved to an area where there were plenty of rocks to hide behind, but nothing to protect them from arrows raining down from above. Harry still hadn't seen Conrad.

I watched as the last of the Indian warriors showed themselves just long enough so the soldiers moved into a different position which was more open for an attack from above. Three of Many Lives' braves were climbing the rock formation Harry was perched on, but they were paying no attention to him, but the soldiers below.

The three made it to the place they had wanted to and for a minute all movement stopped. That's when I recognized one of the three Indians below me was Many Lives himself.

The air was still and quiet, then a loud yip, yip was heard echoing down the rock formation to those below. Moments later the sky was filled with arrows that were set to rain down on the soldiers as they hid behind the rocks thinking themselves safe. Harry could tell this spot had been used before as an ambush spot as the arrows fell with deadly accuracy on the soldiers.

Arrows rained down on the soldiers for what seemed a long time. Harry could see very little movement from below, but heard the sounds of men moaning in pain. As he continued to watch, he saw movement below as one Indian ran into the open to draw any gun fire from the soldiers, there was none.

Below Harry, he heard once again the loud yip, yip and saw at the same time several Indians run amongst the soldiers and kill any that were alive. Many Lives and the two with him moved down the rock formation to join the others below.

Then as Harry watched, Many Lives looked up and in his direction. Many Lives slowly withdrew an arrow from its quiver, strung it on his bow and lifted it up and pointing it directly at Harry and releasing it, set it to flight. A quick flap of Harry's wings put him in flight just as the arrow whizzed past him.

Circling overhead, Harry watched as the soldiers were dragged into an opening between two large boulders where one was pushed away. Once all the dead soldiers were moved to that place, the one boulder was pushed back over the opening, concealing it from sight.

Harry just witnessed twenty soldiers enter Red Rocks and disappear never to be seen or heard from again.

He knew there had to be some logical explanation to the vanishing of anyone who entered Red Rocks, and Harry just witnessed it. He still hadn't seen Conrad and didn't know where he was and why he wasn't there with Harry.

Harry soon became weary of flight and needed to set down and get some needed sleep. Harry had been flying for a long time. Spying a building with an open door, Harry glided down and into it. Finding a comfortable spot, he settled down and fell fast asleep and not wakening till Harry heard the call from the morning rooster and smelled the aroma of fresh boiling coffee.

Chapter 6

You don't look so well, this morning, Harry," the voice of Conrad joining that of the morning rooster.

Sitting up and given off a loud yawning sound, Harry then stood and gave a mighty stretch.

"My, that coffee smells delicious," Harry told Conrad. "Is it ready?"

"Sure is, Harry. Hot and black just as you like it," he said, pouring Harry a cup and handing it to him.

"Molly used to tell me I was a loud snorer, Harry, but your snoring last night woke me up several times."

"Sorry about that, my friend, but I slept through it," a little chuckle sound to his voice brought a smile to Conrad's face.

"Why do you suppose the government decided to send more soldiers after Many Lives when they have asked us to track him down?" asked Conrad.

"I don't know, but when I had contacted the Colonel before, he offered a hand if I needed it. He didn't say anything about going after Many Lives again. Something must have come about for that decision to have been made. Will just have to ask him when he arrives."

As good as the coffee was, it couldn't stem the hunger pangs Harry was feeling at that moment. As much as he wanted to tell Conrad about his dream, right now it was his stomach speaking and it was saying "feed me."

The food was very good at Mandy's Kitchen. For that matter, Mandy was easy to look at also and she visited our table more than you would think. Smiles and light conversation between her and Conrad told Harry something was going on between them.

"You two are getting along nicely," Harry said with a chuckle. "I think she likes you." Drawing a scowl from Conrad's face.

Loud voices were heard. Looking over in the direction they were coming from, both Harry and Conrad saw Mandy in a confrontation with two rough looking cowboys.

Conrad, jumping up from the table, quickly made his way to her side. One of the cowboys seeing him coming, drew his pistol, and before anyone could stop him, shot Conrad in the leg, dropping him to the floor. Seconds later, several of the patrons had jumped in and disarmed the shooter but the damage was done. Conrad had been shot.

Mandy was kneeling beside Conrad who was clutching his leg.

"You'll be okay," Harry heard her tell Conrad.

"Bill, Seth, help get the marshal to Doctor Roberts' office," she instructed two of the patrons. "And on your way back get the sheriff and tell him he needs to get over to Mandy's, pronto."

Helping Conrad to his feet, the two draped his arms around their shoulders and half carried him to the doctor's office. Harry went over and held the shooter till the sheriff arrived, at which time Harry turned him over and left to go to the doctor's office to see how Conrad was.

On the way there, it dawned on him why Conrad hadn't been in his dream. Conrad wasn't there because he couldn't be, he was leg shot and unable to ride. Harry hadn't told Conrad anything about his dream, so when he does, now Harry will have one of the unanswered questions answered. That being, where was Conrad?

Harry found Conrad in the doctor's office. His leg had been bandaged up and he seemed in good spirits for having just been shot. Mandy was at his side.

"The bullet went clear through," Conrad said, the minute Harry walked into the office. "Missed the bone by a fraction of an inch, but I'm afraid I won't be riding no horse for a few days."

"Well, let's get you back to my rail car, we have a lot to talk about," Harry told him.

"Will it be okay if Mandy comes?" he asked, turning to look at her.

"No," Mandy said before Harry could reply. "I can't come with you right now, but I will come by later if that's okay?" she gave Conrad a big smile. "I'll bring some pie."

"That would be very thoughtful," Harry told her. "There will be a number of soldiers here today who I will be leaving with, so Conrad could use the company."

"It's settled then. I'll come by later," giving Conrad a peck on the cheek, Mandy turned and walked from the doctor's office.

The doc gave Conrad a pair of crutches, so he didn't have to put any weight on his injured leg. Although the bullet hadn't hit a bone, it had torn through muscle and that would need time to heal.

Back at Harry's rail car, he had his first coffee making lesson using the new ground coffee he had purchased.

"Well, it smells good," Harry remarked, as the coffee boiled and the steam rose into the air. "Now if it tastes as good as it smells."

For his first pot of coffee, Harry must say it was acceptable. Even Conrad agreed.

As they sat around the table drinking coffee, Harry recanted his dream to Conrad, trying to remember every detail. Afterwards, they sat and discussed the dream and what it meant.

Shortly after, Colonel Pratte arrived with his twenty cavalry soldiers. Harry had described in detail what the

Colonel looked like, right down to the rust colored mare he rode upon.

Wanting to get underway, Harry bid farewell to Conrad, knowing if his dream was accurate, Harry would be returning. He would have a chance to share his dream with the Colonel on the trail, if Harry determined the Colonel would listen and not think Harry some kind of fool. And it didn't take him long to know that is exactly what the Colonel would think, but still, Harry would share it with him when the time was right.

Harry was told that the reason the army was going after Many Lives, instead of waiting to see how Harry made out in capturing him, was there had been another settler's homestead attacked and all were killed, including the five children, who also showed signs of mutilation.

The little town of Bale, Nebraska was up in arms over it and had wired the governor, who had even wired the president, and in turn he had contacted the commanders at both Fort Omaha and Fort Kearney. Fort Omaha, being the closest, got the orders to track down and at any cost bring down this renegade Indian Many Lives and his band of savages.

As they rode onto Red Rocks, Harry couldn't stop thinking how things had come about so far and if somehow he had traveled into the spirit world and been given a glimpse of events to come. Then they were riding into a well set trap that would result in the death of the Colonel and all his soldiers.

Before they arrived at Red Rocks, Harry did share his dream with the colonel and as suspected it was hog wash and he wasn't about to listen to anything Harry had to tell him.

"If you don't want to believe me, at least keep your eye out for the signs I told you about," Harry warned. "Don't be close minded, you and your soldier's lives depend on it," Harry told him. But by the Colonel's facial expressions, Harry knew he wasn't taking what Harry was telling him seriously.

Reining up just outside of the entrance to Red Rocks, Colonel Pratte gave the orders to enter and shoot straight. Turning to Harry, he told him to stay put. He didn't want to be responsible for Harry's life.

As he and his soldiers rode away, Harry felt saddened knowing what was about to take place.

Eagle, watching from above, rock formation! These words invaded Harry's mind and at once it also screamed, follow the signs. Scanning the horizon, Harry saw the exact rock formation from his dream. Galloping to it, he dismounted and started to climb to the top.

Once there, Harry was able to overlook the whole area below. Movement caught his eye and Harry saw the colonel and the soldiers riding into the clearing in the rocks below. Other movement caught his attention and sure enough just like in his dream, Many Lives' warriors had started the job of dividing the troops in two.

Remembering his dream, Harry looked immediately below him, amazed to see Many Lives and two other braves making their way up the rock formation he was huddled on top of. If the real does mirror his dream, Harry knew that he wouldn't be found out, but Many Lives would stop short of coming all the way to the top. Then, as in the dream, Many Lives sounded a loud yip, yip, and when he had, a storm of arrows were launched into the sky to rain down on the unsuspecting soldiers.

As in Harry's dream, the battle was short lived. Another yip, yip and he witnessed the Indian warriors move about the soldiers who lay injured taking their lives.

Knowing that Many Lives was going to look up at any minute and see Harry, he crawled back down the way he came up. Not sure exactly what was going to happen next, because in his dream Harry simple flew away.

If Many Lives was having the same sort of dreams, does he know I'm up here? Does he know where I'm going to go to get out of here? Harry's thoughts were great and racing back and forth inside his head.

Stopping Harry's mind from racing, he stopped and revisited his dream.

In his dream, Many Lives saw Harry and fired an arrow at him, which whizzed past as Harry took to the air. He then went back to celebrating with his warriors and ignored Harry altogether. Taking his dream to task, Harry continued down the rock formation, found his horse, and rode away from Red Rocks and the death that was there, knowing Many Lives would be once again tracked by the government soldiers till he was captured or killed.

If the government went that route, Harry's assignment might be over. In his dream as an eagle, Harry made it safely back to Dusty Hollow so he wasn't much worried now about making it back.

The ride out with the soldiers had been a tough one. They were used to being in the saddle for hours on end. Harry, not so much, and now his body ached all over.

No coffee tonight. This one thought kept running through Harry's mind. *It's funny when you want something and can't get it, how that's all you can think about. I knew what was going to happen so I was nuts not to plan on it and bring some provisions with me.*

His plan was to ride through the night, that way he should be back in Dusty Hollow tomorrow early afternoon, if in reality he could stay in the saddle that long. As Harry rode, his sensors picked up the smell of smoke. A little hesitation from his horse told Harry that he had smelled the smoke also.

Reining his horse to a stop, Harry looked around the landscape to see if he could see any whisper of smoke which would tell him where a camp might be set up. Spying the smoke, Harry made his way over to it, calling out as he did. After all, he didn't want to get shot.

Being invited in by the camp patron, Harry got down from his horse and introduced himself as US Marshal Harry Finch.

"Marshal, I'm Scott Parker. Interest you in a cup of Joe?" he asked, extending his hand.

"Don't need to be asking me twice," Harry told him, reaching for the cup Scott held out to Harry.

"Much appreciated," Harry said. "It's been a long, hard day."

It has been a long day thinking about all that had gone on and troubled by so many deaths just because a Colonel didn't believe, now twenty young brave soldiers are being dragged into a cave never to be seen again.

Coffee was good and so was the company.

Scott was from NY and headed west to California.

"What in tar nation are you crossing the plains by yourself for? Don't you read the papers? Don't you know the white man is still at war with the Indian?" Harry wanted to tell him about the day's happenings but couldn't, instead Harry invited him to come back to Dusty Hollow.

"I appreciate your concern and your offer," he replied. "But I need to get to California."

"You're not going to make it son," Harry tried to tell him. Harry actually thought about arresting him in order to save his life but he didn't. *If he wants to kill himself go ahead and let him,* were Harry's thoughts.

"You're headed into a war party of Indians. If California is worth your life, you have at it, but you should come back with me and wait for a wagon train or at least the next military escort or tomorrow will be your last day alive."

"You can't scare me, marshal. I'm going to California. Made it this far."

I've always liked a man with determination, but not the kind that will get yourself or others injured. I saw that with the colonel today and he's dead, and now you will be also.

Draining his coffee cup, Harry wished this young man good luck and headed out. It would be dark soon and he still had a long ride. While the trail was still light, Harry edged his mount into a medium trot.

It actually felt good to be on the trail by himself, listening to the creaking of the saddle, the steady thud, thud of horse shoe meeting the hard trail. The slight breeze in your face as you cut through the air.

Harry wasn't concerned about being followed by Many Lives. He and his warriors were well into celebrating the great victory they enjoyed against the soldiers, today.

There was no way of knowing how many soldiers Many Lives actually killed that day, so to figure how many new scalps he would be adding to his collection was a guess. Harry's thoughts as he rode into the night.

I wonder how Conrad is? Was his next thought. *At least the bullet had missed the bone that would have laid him up for a good long time and rendered him just about useless for this assignment. As it is, he should be okay in a couple of days if infection don't set in. There will be some pain but he can handle it.*

Harry was trying to think of other things instead of the day's happenings, and not only that, but how everything mirrored his dream.

Harry knew he didn't have any answers and there were lots of unanswered questions.

As soon as I get back, I need to wire the office in DC and get some direction into this matter of the supernatural and why is it I'm experiencing this.

Thank god there's a bright moon out tonight. Harry thought as he rode. The trail was almost as visible as it is in the day light, which ended his earlier concern about riding it in the dark.

Stopping to give his backside a short rest, Harry looked out over the open plain lit with the silvery glow from the moon and the millions of stars which created a blanket over the earth.

Harry had never been one to give thought to the hereafter, or a GOD as most people, including his wife Amanda, believed in.

Gazing into the heavens and out across the plain, he had to admit it did seem possible that something made all he was looking at, that it hadn't just happened.

"What do you think, boy," Harry asked his horse. "Is there a God, you think?" A couple slaps on his neck created a small puff of trail dust.

"Maybe I need to speak with a pastor or a reverend when we get back to Dusty Hollow, what do you think, boy?"

Harry's answer was a loud snort followed by a little nickering sound.

"I guess if I'm going to be out on the trail this much, I need to have my Buck here," Harry said speaking to the horse as if he was another person.

"You'd like Buck. You two are pretty much the same." More nickering told Harry that it was time to move on.

As he rode on, he thought how he would approach his boss to arrange for a horse car so whenever he had to be on the trail, he could take along his own horse.

If he couldn't talk his boss into that, at least he had to remember to take along his own saddle. This one was a shy small for him and had just started to rub his tailbone area.

"I can feel a saddle sore coming on," he said out loud. Stepping down into the stirrups he was able to take some of his weight off his tailbone, but knew it was only temporary as he couldn't continue riding that way. Stopping, Harry dismounted and removed his vest and folded it up to make a pad for his backside.

"There," he said sitting back in the saddle, feeling better with the extra padding from his vest.

Soon the sun started to rise in the east and Harry could make out some buildings telling him he was just about to Dusty Hollow.

Coffee, food, bath. All in that order was what was on Harry's mind as he rode into town.

Chapter 7

With coffee, food, and a bath out of the way, Harry made his way to his rail car where he found Conrad and Mandy laughing and seemly enjoying each other's company.

"Well, will you look whose back," said Conrad, as Harry stepped into his rail car.

"Fresh pot on the stove, Harry." Conrad motioned in the direction of the stove, getting up he extended his hand in welcome.

"You seem to be moving okay," Harry said to Conrad. "Legs healing pretty quickly I see."

"Mandy's been taking real good care of me since you've been gone." Conrad sensing something wrong asked. "Where are the soldiers you left with?"

Over coffee, Harry told the story of the massacre of Colonel Pratte and his cavalry.

After telling in detail of the demise of the colonel, Harry told of the young Scott Parker who Harry had met on the trail. How he had tried to talk him out of continuing his journey, but it was to no avail.

"He was determined to go to California and nothing I told him was going to change his mind, not even when I told him he would be dead tomorrow."

Tomorrow, he would be riding right by Many Lives home alone, just wanting to go to California, something he should be able to do without worry of being killed by savage Indians.

"Can you ride?" Harry asked. "If you can, let's go." Harry knew what he had to do even if fruitless.

"Where to Harry?" asked Conrad, getting to his feet.

"To save a young man and put an end to the Indian Many Lives' reign of death for anyone entering his land. And if we ride hard, we might be able to catch up with him."

Harry knew this would probably be a worthless cause, but needed to do something. his assignment was to capture Many Lives and that is what he intended to do.

Harry sent a telegraph out to the commander at Fort Kearney advising him of the massacre of Colonel Pratte and twenty of his soldiers and the location Many Lives calls home.

"Tell me Harry. If the happenings were the same as in your dream, why didn't you shoot Many Lives when you had a chance to?" Conrad asked. "You said he was right below you on the rock formation."

"I couldn't," Harry answered him, "I couldn't draw my pistol or pick up my rifle. The only thing I can attribute that to is an eagle can't fire a gun so neither was I able to fire a weapon. No matter how hard I tried, I just couldn't."

I wonder what would have happened if I would have let the dream play out by letting Many Lives see me, I wonder if he would have shot an arrow at me like in the dream. Another question I needed to get answered.

"I think you have a gift Harry and should find out all you can concerning it. Because of your dream you are alive today. If Many Lives would have seen you, you know what would have happened," Conrad told me. "Colonel Pratte and those twenty soldiers would be alive today if the colonel would have listened to you, but he didn't."

"You're right, Conrad, but who can help me understand this gift, if it really is one," he asked, wanting to know more.

"I've got it!" exclaimed Conrad. "You need to speak to a spiritual leader of an Indian tribe. He would be able to tell you. He could probably bless you with knowledge of the Spirit World so you can better understand future dreams."

Excited now to learn more about the Spirit World and a better understanding of his dreams, Harry needed to find a spiritual leader of an Indian tribe.

"About a half day's ride north of here is a Cheyenne Reservation and I would guess there is a spiritual leader there. It is a very large Indian encampment," he continued. "We could head there, but that would mean your trail friend is on his own."

"There was little hope in catching him before Many Lives did, besides this is more important. What if Many Lives had this same gift but could read it better? He would know in advance how a battle would turn out so he could make adjustments and he could put himself and his warriors out of danger, sorta making himself invincible in advance," Harry told him. "Just like I knew Many Lives would look up and see me in advance, so that I hid myself at the right moment so he didn't see me, thus saving my life."

"Makes sense, Harry. Let's head north and see if we can get some answers before we encounter Many Lives again. Let's talk with the sheriff here and ask him about the tribe north of here, and wire the commander at Fort Kearney again and ask him also. You haven't heard back from him yet anyways."

"No I haven't. In conversation with Colonel Pratte, I learned about another regiment of soldiers at a Fort Leavenworth in Kansas," Harry told Conrad. "Have you heard of it?"

Seeing Conrad's eye brows lift in recognition at the mention of Fort Leavenworth, Harry wondered what he was going to answer.

"Yes Harry, I've heard of this Fort," he said. "Want another coffee before I begin?"

"No thanks, Conrad. Let's hear what you know."

"Well, I don't know the commanders name but, Fort Leavenworth is a colored regiment of soldiers, referred to by the Comanche Indians as Wild Buffalo, a name the Apache also called them because of their kinky, curly, black hair which resembled the hide of a buffalo. This name got changed by the white man to Buffalo Soldier in reference to their black skin. Ever hear of them?"

"I have. But I don't know anything about them," Harry told Conrad. "Who's their commander?"

"I don't know," he said.

"Maybe I can find out before I make contact with them," Harry mentioned. "Don't suppose Mandy would know, do you?" Harry asked, turning to face her.

"Today is your lucky day in more ways than one," she said. "Yes, I do know, his name is David Mathis. Stout guy, polite. A real gentleman," she told them. "Makes it into my place about once a month when he performs his duty and visits all the reservations in his jurisdiction. He should be coming by just about any day now," she told me.

Mandy hadn't any more than said that, when they all heard the sound of many horses stomping the ground and followed by a loud resounding, company halt. This followed by another loud command, company dismount.

"Looks like today really is your lucky day, Harry," she said.

Looking out the rail car windows, Harry was astonished at the sight that greeted his eyes, for he had never seen a black man wearing the uniform, never mind a whole company of them.

He guessed what stuck out the most for him as he stood staring out at them, was Commander David Mathis was white. Harry guessed it just figured Mathis would also be colored.

"That's him," Mandy said, pointing to the white man. "That's David Mathis."

It was easy to see that they were well known in town, as several of the town's people went up and greeted them.

"Well boys, you'll have to excuse me now," said Mandy. "Drop by my place in twenty minutes and I'll introduce you to Commander Mathis."

"That would be great, Mandy. I'd appreciate that." Harry told her.

"And you, take care of yourself," she said to Conrad giving him a light kiss in the cheek. "I'll see you later."

With that, Mandy was gone.

Harry watched as she hurriedly left and went to greet Commander Mathis. Harry saw his face light up when Mathis saw Mandy walking his way.

Mandy was right. Commander Mathis was a gentleman. For as Harry watched, Mathis extended his arm, which she wrapped hers through and together they headed for her place, to get coffee and maybe pie, Harry surmised.

"Relax," Harry told Conrad seeing his long face as he too watched them walk arm an arm down the street.

"Let's have a coffee, then we'll go over to Mandy's and meet the commander and see what answers he can supply us with."

Twenty minutes later, they were walking through the door to Mandy's Kitchen and some sought after answers. In the corner by himself sat Commander Mathis who Harry walked right over to, followed by Conrad.

Commander Mathis," Harry asked as he approached his table. "I'm US Marshal Harry Finch and this is my partner US Marshal Conrad Johnson. Do you have a couple of minutes for us?" Harry asked.

Nodding for them to sit, he responded to Harry's introduction.

"Oh, yes. Mandy told me I might expect two US Marshal," he said, extending his hand in greeting. "I'm General David Mathis and I am the commander of Fort Leavenworth in Kansas. Now, how can I help you?" he asked. "Mandy told me you wanted some information on the Cheyenne reservation just north of here?"

Mandy showed up with a coffee pot and cups.

"Anything you need, just let me know," she told them, sat the cups in front of them, poured the cups to the brim with the hot, black liquid and left.

"So, marshal, what can I do for you?" he asked after taking a sip of coffee.

"Well General, first let me fill you in on what I have witnessed the past couple of days." Harry told him the story of the demise of Colonel Pratte and his soldiers. He listened with intense interest, but you could read the sadness, then anger, in his face.

"I have gone after this Many Lives in the past but he has always evaded capture. I followed him into an area known as Red Rocks, but realized how quickly we could become trapped in this maze."

"It's a good thing you cut to the chase. Red Rocks is where I witnessed the massacre of the Colonel and his troops," Harry told him. That is Many Lives' home ground and he knows it like the back of his hand."

"I appreciate all this information, now, you wanted to ask me something?" the General questioned.

"Well General, I hope you don't think me nuts by what I'm going to share with you. It might sound unreal, but if that Colonel Pratte would have believed me, I think he would be alive today."

As Harry spoke he noticed the General slide a little forward in his chair.

He's listening to me, Harry thought.

"Please continue," he said. "What you're saying sounds intriguing."

"To make a long story short," *here it comes General,* was his last thought. "I had a dream."

Noticing the raised eyebrows and a slight tip of the general's head, I continued.

"I've had a couple of dreams and a very unusual happening and I don't understand what it all means," Harry continued.

He went on to explain in detail the happenings at Red Rocks, the arrows and the thunder, the bolt of lightning, and the arrow turning to dust.

Not once during all of Harry's story did the General interrupt me, instead he sat with an intense look on his face for most of the story. He did frown a couple of times when he heard something he couldn't understand.

"Looks like you two need another pot of coffee," Mandy' voice interrupted.

"Sounds good Mandy, and some pie," it was the general who spoke. "You will have some, won't you Marshal?"

"Coffee and pie, the heart blood of the west, isn't that what they say?" Harry asked, a slight smile on his face.

"I wasn't going after Many Lives, but hearing your story it looks like I have to and once and for all, put an end to this renegade Indian."

"I need your help general," Harry blurted out. "But I need to ask a question first."

Looking the general in the eye, Harry asked, "Do you believe my story about the dreams, do you believe in the Spirit World, and the belief we can look into the future?"

"I head up a fort of colored men. Some believe as most, but some have beliefs in the supernatural. "I've sat with my men around the campfire and heard their stories," he said, stopping only to sip his coffee.

"Although I find their stories of the supernatural fascinating and some unbelievable, doesn't make them any less truthful. They believe in them, which in their eyes make them true. Just as the Indian have their Medicine Men and spiritual leaders to believe in and seek guidance from, they have their gods."

"This last dream was so real. The massacre that took place mirrored it. Because I had seen the ending, is why I am alive and here today. I was able to change the ending. I need to know what I can do or how I can read my dreams in the future if I have another one," Harry said.

"How can I help you, I'm no spiritual being. I have no super powers."

"I know. But you know the spiritual leader in the Indian reservation at Two Pines north of here. Could you go there with me and represent me. I understand the Indians there have a lot of respect for you and your colored soldiers."

"They do," he told Harry, but it's because I extend that same respect and understanding back to them. We took their land. How would you feel if your land was taken?"

There was quietness at their table for several minutes before the general continued speaking.

Harry didn't know why, several days ago, he woke up with a strong desire to visit the reservation at Two Pines. After all, it is a long ride, but he was being drawn like a magnet. Now Harry knew why that was. If you do have the ability to dream into the future the spiritual leader at Two Pines will be the Indian who can help you understand.

As they got up to leave, General Mathis instructed Harry to meet him in the morning at a place called Lizard Lick, that is where they would camp the night.

Thanking the general, Harry assured him both Conrad and he would meet the general in the morning at this place called Lizard Lick.

Strange name, Harry thought to himself. *Lizard Lick. Can only guess why it's called that.*

Returning to his rail car, Harry found Conrad lying in his bunk.

"How's the leg?" Harry asked him. "Think you're up for a ride in the morning?"

"Sure am Harry, where we headed? To the reservation?"

"Yup, leaving first light. The general told me he would get us there and vouch for me with their chief and spiritual leader," Harry told him. "And he also believes in things unexplained.

"I found out the tribe there is Cheyenne and their chief only wants to live in peace. He is old and no longer wants to be at war with the white man. He has lost many young braves. They have removed their war paints and have a special bond with this general who leads a bunch of colored soldiers.

"The general told me their spiritual leader's name was Eyes into the Future. Strange name but General Mathis told me he can interrupt dreams and he can also direct me in acceptance to them."

"What else did you find out from the general?" Conrad asked. Limping to the stove he also asked, "Want some coffee, Harry?"

As good as a cup of coffee would be, Harry told him no.

"We both need to get some sleep. The morning will be here before we know it and I want to be alert tomorrow."

Secretly, Harry wanted to get to sleep and see if he would have any dreams that he could share tomorrow, so he could better understand them.

As soon as his eyes shut and sleep came over him, the dreams started.

Conrad and I were on horseback riding with General Mathis and his Buffalo Soldiers as they were known by the Indian. We had gone to see the spiritual leader known by the name Eyes into the Future and I had told him about a dream I had.

Now we were headed to Red Rocks with the general. No one talked as we rode. The creaking of the saddles and the constant clomp, clomp of horse shoes against the hard trail were the only sounds heard.

As abruptly as my dream started, it ended. I immediately found myself transported to Red Rocks where a battle was taking place between some other soldiers. These soldiers being all white.

As in the last dream, I once again took the form of an Eagle sitting atop the rock formation looking down into the Indian-staged battlefield at the unsuspecting soldiers, unaware of the hell that was soon to rain down on them from the sky.

There below me in the same place was Many Lives and two warriors watching the happenings below, waiting for the right moment to invade the sky with their weapons of death.

Below, I saw who must be the soldier's leader. He was running from area to area where his soldiers were grouped ready to take on Many Lives, still unaware of what was to come from above.

Deciding this time not to let the soldiers be surprised from above, just as Many Lives raised his bow and launched the first arrow into the sky, signaling the attack to begin, I gave out a mighty screech of warning!

Heeeeeeeeaaahhh, squaaaaaaaaaaa, heeeeeeeeeeeeeaaahhh. I continued.

As the sky came alive with arrows, so did the soldiers look up and saw the arrows that would soon rain down onto them. I watched them all dive for some different cover. Cover that offered them protection from this onslaught of arrows from the sky. I took flight to avoid the cylinders of death with the three red circles painted in their centers, which I knew would be fired in my direction.

Looking down as I circled above, I didn't see one wounded soldier. Then I was circling over another group of soldiers.

These soldiers were as dark as the night's sky being led by a very distinguished looking office who I recognized as General Davis Mathis. On his left and his right rode two other white figures. Oh look! It's Conrad and I!

Chapter 8

Awakening the next morning, Harry lay in his bunk and recalled the dream of last night. He had wondered why he couldn't get in contact with Lieutenant Hastings from Fort Kearney, now Harry knew why. It was due to the fact he was at Red Rocks at this very moment under attack from Many Lives and his renegades.

The room was filled with the aroma of boiling coffee. Swinging his legs out of bed and sitting up, Conrad handed Harry a cup filled to the brim with the hot, black liquid he was addicted to.

"I was just going to wake you Harry," he said. "We have to be headed out to meet the general."

Having the facilities right there was convenient. No time to get to Mandy's for breakfast, so draining his cup, Harry was ready to ride. The knock on the door was answered by Conrad.

"Our horses are here," he informed Harry. "Saddled and ready to go."

Conrad and Harry rode in haste to get to Lizard Lick and meet General Mathis. From there on to the reservation and hopefully a meeting with their Spiritual Leader, Eyes into the Future.

Conrad's leg didn't seem to bother him and soon we arrived at Lizard Lick, where we found the general and his men all saddled up and ready to ride.

"Mount them up corporal, and let's ride," he instructed his second in command.

As we rode, Harry shared his dream with the general, who listened intensely when Harry got to the part where the soldiers came under attack.

"You saw them under attack?" he questioned back.

"Yes I did. As I mentioned in my dream, I warned them just in time to the incoming arrows from above. From the position where Many Lives attacked, he couldn't attack in any other way without being in the direct line of the soldier's rifles," Harry told him. "Many Lives never planned on anyone surviving his onslaught from above, so now he wasn't able to attack differently."

"How long do you think they can survive there?" the general asked.

"As long as they stay where they are and not try to advance and attack the Indians, they will be fine," Harry assured him. "How well do you know the Lieutenant from Fort Kearney?" Harry asked.

"I know him well. We have fought many a campaign together. He won't do anything foolish," he told Harry.

The smell of smoke told him they were arriving at the Indian reservation at Two Pines. The reservation at Two Pines wasn't anything like Harry had expected.

For starters, it was a very large community of Indians. Along with the teepees there were a lot of wooden building housing many of the shops and businesses any town would have.

Two Pines was more of an Indian town then an Indian reservation. It was even laid out like a white man's town. Riding through town, Harry was aware every Indian was staring at them. Eyes followed, untrusting in their facial features. To Harry's surprise, the short hairs on his neck weren't jumping up and down in warning.

Just the other side of town were the teepees. This was more a picture of what Harry had an Indian reservation looking like. He could see they were headed for a brightly decorated teepee that had all kinds of artifacts outside of it, and many paintings covered the white skins which made up the teepee.

Gazing at the teepee next to this one, Harry took to be the Indian's Medicine Man. This teepee was surrounded by the skulls of dead animals, buffalo, elk, bear, wolf, and deer, in some cases more than one.

Reining up in front of what Harry surmised as the teepee belonging to the Spiritual Leader, General Mathis cupped his hands around his mouth and gave off a low sounding wolf call.

"Awoooooo, aww, aww, awoooooo," he called out. "Awooooooooo."

The flap covering the teepee entrance was flipped open. Harry watched as three little Indian children emerged followed by a young Indian woman who he figured was the children's mother. Looking closely, she appeared to be with child again.

Next to emerge was a gray haired squaw woman. She wore pure white skins decorated with colorful feathers and beads. Bracelets of silver and gem stones. Her face was painted most beautifully.

Next out of the teepee was the Indian Spiritual Leader known as Eyes into the Future.

If a picture could be painted to represent a Spiritual Leader, it would be one of this Indian who stood in front of his teepee, Harry thought.

Eyes into the Future also wore skins of pure white, so white they gave off a seemingly halo of white all around him. *He glows,* were Harry's thoughts. He too, was adorned with all kinds of colorful feathers, beads, and silver ornaments. He wore no face paint.

The general stepped down off his mount and motioned for Harry to follow, which he did. Standing directly in front of this Indian, he extended his arm which Eyes into the Future grasped with his own. This was his way of greetings.

Harry was surprised when the general turned towards him and in English introduced Harry. This introduction was also followed by an extended arm.

"My dear friend," said the general. "Can we have some time with you? It is of the utmost importance."

Turning, this great leader indicated for them to enter his home.

The three sat cross legged on another pure white skin, one of many covering the floor.

"What can I do for you?" he asked. Then asked if he could get them something to eat or drink.

"No thank you," the general said. "I need you to help the US Marshal with dreams he has been having that also mirror happenings in the real world."

Turning to Harry then back to him, the general continued.

"He had a dream last night and now we think lots of soldiers are about to be killed by a renegade warrior by the name of Many Lives."

The name Many Lives raised the Spiritual Leaders eye brows.

With eyes lowered, he whispered, "My son."

Silence followed and Harry thought their conversation would be ended, but the head was lifted and he asked, "How can I help?"

About an hour later, Conrad, the general, myself and his regiment of black soldiers were riding towards Red Rocks knowing it wasn't too late to join Lieutenant Hastings and his soldiers, who were held down by Many Lives and his warriors.

Nothing more was mentioned about Many Lives being the son of Eyes into the Future.

We will need to ride through the night if we are to be of help to them. Tomorrow would be three days they would be held down. Did they have any provisions, water? We didn't know. If only I could go to sleep and dream some more, maybe I could learn what was going on at Red Rocks, Harry thought.

As they rode, something the Spirit Leader had said. "You don't have to dream to look into the future. All you need to do is detach yourself from your inner being and surroundings. Think deep about what you want to have knowledge about."

As night engulfed us, Harry let the darkness block out all things around him.

The creaking of the saddles and the constant drumming of the horse's hooves soon had Harry mesmerized and he was no longer on a horse racing into the night, but now an owl.

Time was nonexistent as I was transported above Red Rocks and sat down on the large rock formation to observe the area below.

I observed Many Lives and his warriors launch a few arrows into the night sky having tied material around their tips and sat them afire. Landing among the soldiers and lighting up the area until they burned out or one of the men ran out and stomped it out.

The men appeared weak. No water I observed. There was a small watering hole nearby, but Many Lives had placed a couple of warriors there, just in case the soldiers were to locate it.

Swooping down to a tree above where Many Lives had made his camp, I listened to his plan to attack the soldiers at the height of the day, when the heat had drained the remainder of liquid from their bodies and they were at their weakest. Armed with this information I spread my wings and took to flight, flying as fast as I could as it was getting to be daylight.

As the first slivers of the golden sun pierced the eastern sky, I found myself back in the saddle. At the first loud snort from my mount, I was awakened from the trance-like state I had been in.

They're alive," Harry blurted out. "I saw them and they are alive."

"Welcome back, Harry," it was Conrad's voice. "Sorry, but I don't have any coffee made. I told the General when you came back from wherever you were, you would be needing a coffee, but he wasn't hearing me. Maybe now he will stop long enough to boil a pot and let the men get some grub, after all, if they are going to be engaged in a battle, they should do so on full stomachs, don't you think?"

"We do have enough time to get some grub and a cup of coffee boiled," Harry told the general. "Everyone has been riding hard and a thirty-minute break will be welcomed, and I can tell you all about what I saw during the night, while I was at Red Rocks."

Orders were given and a thirty-minute break was commanded. Harry couldn't believe that here was an army general actually listening to a civilian. Harry would be sure to inform the general's commander of his great abilities as a general.

Cupping a hot coffee cup in his hands, Harry told the general all he had seen. Harry told him where the Indians were hidden, where Many Lives' main camp was, and what his plans of attack were.

"When we get to Red Rocks, you should send several men to release the Indian ponies which will give you the advantage over them. They will be on foot, you will attack on horseback."

"When we get to where you want us to be, say the word and I will see to it any instructions you have for us will be followed."

So far General Mathis had listened to my every word. We will be victorious here today. Harry thought, draining his cup and indicating to the general it was time to ride.

He gave the order to "mount-up" and followed by, "Company Forward."

As they rode, Harry tried to think what else the Spiritual Leader had shared with him concerning the Spirit World and what was possible to do while a visitor in it.

Harry knew it was possible to call out a warning, as he had done so earlier while as an eagle, warning the soldiers to look up, but now Harry wanted to advise them help was on the way.

How can I do that, he thought.

The Spiritual Leader had told Harry that, *while in the Spirit World, you can do whatever the form of animal or bird you took on can do in the real world.*

What can an owl do? Harry's thoughts took over and his mind started racing at the speed of light, searching for an answer.

His thoughts suddenly halted. There it was. The answer he was searching for.

"General," Harry said getting his attention. "I need you to write down a quick note that help is on the way, and give me an item Lieutenant Hastings will recognize to make the note more believable."

"What are you going to do?" Conrad asked.

The general halted the troops and started his note.

"I can bring him a note," Harry told him. "An owl could grasp an item in its claw and deliver it to the lieutenant," Harry told him.

"An owl?" he questioned. "Why an owl?"

"Absolutely! Why an owl? An eagle will travel faster."

"Here you go, Marshal," General Mathis said. As he handed Harry the note, the general reached up and removed one of his bars from his uniform. "He'll recognize that." the general told Harry, handing to Harry his uniform bar.

"Conrad, I need you to come with me now," Harry said. Turning towards the general, Harry told him to take a few minutes break and let Conrad and Harry go on alone a ways, so Harry could be less distracted and be able to enter the Spirit World more easily.

"Pass the word to take ten," he instructed his next in command. All stepped down and stood next to their mounts.

"Let's go," Harry said. Putting heel to flank, his mount leaped forward at a quick pace, Conrad by Harry's side. Pulling way ahead of the troops, Harry slowed down and told Conrad to take Harry's reins and just make sure he follows.

"I want to shut my eyes as we ride and concentrate on the Spirit World," Harry told him. "I need to put myself in a state of complete relaxation."

Shutting his eyes, Harry listened to the constant clack, clickity clack, and clickity clack of the hooves making contact with the ground.

The sound was mesmerizing and soon he was an eagle racing over the plains, his eyes unblinking, focused on one thing.

Remember, whatever form you take on, you can do whatever it is capable of doing in the real world. Harry thought. These words from Eyes into the Future came back to Harry and he decided if possible, he would fly right up next to the lieutenant and set down next to him, just about handing him the package in person.

Harry chose to land atop the rock formation first to scan the area and locate the lieutenant. He could see lots of movement in Many Lives' camp as they readied themselves for battle. There was much gaiety in his camp brought on by the approaching battle and assured victory.

This battle will be different, Harry thought.

Looking down into the area where the soldiers were huddled, Harry saw the lieutenant. He was carefully going from area to area checking on his men.

Boy, was he in for a surprise, Harry thought.

Clutching both note and shoulder bar in his claw, he lifted off, spread his wings and noiselessly glided down, and to the lieutenant's utter amazement, landed next to him.

Startled momentarily, the lieutenant shrugged back away from Harry, then caught Harry's eyes and followed them down until they were focused on the note Harry had brought and the uniform bar.

Making eye contact one last time with the lieutenant, Harry lifted off leaving his delivery.

Harry hadn't escaped the eyes of Many Lives though, and an arrow whizzed pass his head. His flight was suddenly frozen and Harry was stopped in mid-air, suspended so it seemed by some invisible force.

Turning his head in the direction the arrow had come from and looking down, Harry saw him. Many Lives was standing up-right, his arm extended above his head, bow in hand. He had just released the arrow that whizzed past Harry's head.

Although Harry couldn't move, he was able to turn his head, and in doing so, he watched as the lieutenant picked up the note and opened it.

His eye movement told Harry he was reading the written words from the general.

Next, Harry saw him pick up the general's uniform bar.

I continued watching as he set the two items down and started running amongst his troops. Seeing the looks on their faces, Harry knew for sure the items were believed and they were aware of the arriving help.

Turning his head back to gaze down once again at Many Lives, their eyes met and instantly no distance separated them. They seemed locked together, frozen in the moment, staring eye to eye. Then his eyes changed and in that instant Harry knew!

Many Lives had recognized Harry. No, not as US Marshal Harry Finch, but as a traveler in the Spirit World.

Chapter 9

"You're back," were the first words Harry heard in returning to the real world. These two simple words he would come to cherish in the future. They meant he was back into the real world. Traveling in the Spirit World, Harry still wasn't sure about everything that could transpire there.

If I could travel in the Spirit World, witness the happenings, then return and be able to change the outcome, could I be changed? Could I be killed? Could I be frozen in the Spirit World never to return? Questions unanswered! But not to think about now.

"How did you know?" Harry asked Conrad. "Did I give off some kind of sign?" he questioned.

"Your body shook," he told Harry. "Just like a wet dog shaking off all that wetness."

"It must have been your spirit body joining back with your real body," he surmised.

"Let's go inform the general," Harry told him, turning his horse around and racing back to the column of soldiers to inform General Mathis of his success in contacting the lieutenant.

The general saw them from a distance and ordered a halt to his troops. They sat upon their mounts and watched as Harry and Conrad galloped up.

General Mathis gave an audible sigh of relief when told the lieutenant obviously believed the note as Harry watched him running from one group of soldiers to the next giving them the information from Mathis' note and showing them his uniform bar.

"Although I heard Many Lives tell his warriors they would wait till noon day to attack, he might change his mind right after he saw me and shot an arrow at me. It missed me, but something strange happened. As I looked down to see who fired the arrow at me, I made eye contact with Many Lives. When I did, all of time stopped, and I was frozen in flight, suspended in air," Harry told them. "Everything around us was also frozen, unmoving," he relayed to them, hoping they believed.

"As I continued looking into Many Lives' eyes, I saw them getting larger and larger, I thought they were going to pop right out from their sockets. Then I saw his lips move and heard his whispered voice say, *yadalanh Ka Dish Day.*

"What does that mean," asked Conrad.

"It means, farewell, we will meet again," it was General Mathis who spoke. "He recognized you as a being in the Spirit World, and to do that, he had to have been in the Spirit World. Isn't that what we were told by the Spirit leader, Eyes into the Future?"

"It is just what we were told," Harry whispered. "And he is correct, we will meet again."

"We need to be riding, the lieutenant is expecting us." Harry told them. "And I have a rendezvous to keep with Many Lives."

The remainder of the ride to Red Rocks was done swiftly and uneventfully. The general and his troops were accustomed to riding hard and the terrain passed by in a blur. Soon they were gathered at the entrance of Red Rocks where they heard some rifle fire.

Harry was hoping to have some time to see if he could enter the Spirit World and see where Many Lives and his warriors were so the army would know, but the gun fire told them they were out of time and needed to act now. Dismounting, Harry indicated for the general to observe what Harry was drawing in the dirt.

"Here is the pass we will ride through to enter Red Rocks. And here is what it will look like as soon as we enter, and here, here, and here are the spots I last observed Lieutenant Hastings men were," these areas Harry marked with an 'X.'

"Here is the large rock formation you can see right over there," Harry said pointing in its direction.

This rock formation towered above the whole Red Rocks area and Harry had decided Conrad and he would go there.

"And here are the areas I last saw Many Lives and his warriors. As you can see, he can't attack without running smack dab in front of the lieutenant's men but, if he was to go around this area here, he could actually come up behind them, and that is what I think he will do."

"What do you suppose the men in there are shooting at?" asked Conrad.

"Probably Many Lives has a couple of his warriors running around from rock to rock and tree to tree to keep their attention while he leads the rest of his braves around the flats emerging here where I said he might."

"Considering you are right in your assumption, Many Lives will circle around here," said the general making more marks in the dirt.

"I think I should send in maybe ten soldiers here, and take the rest and circle around here and meet him head on," the general said. Indicating what he was saying by drawing it out.

"If you are right in thinking there are only two or three Indians left here, between my ten, and the soldiers there, it should be easy to overtake them even if they can fire their arrows from a longer distance away. They were more prepared to deliver their arrows from the sky, not head on. That will leave me the remainder of my troops to engage Many Lives here."

Following his plan as he mapped it out in the dirt, Harry agreed it looked like a solid plan and one that should have the element of surprise to it.

"They won't be expecting any other troops," Harry told him.

"Take a walk over here with me, marshal. I need to speak with you in private," General Mathis asked.

Once he was sure we were out of hearing distance, he stopped and asked Harry about Many Lives.

"You know, there have been a lot of stories told about this Indian we know as Many Lives. My men have spoken of him in the past. As many of us as there are, my men are worried. I haven't seen them as worried about an impending battle as they are now," he told Harry.

"Look at them. I haven't seen one of them smile since we left the fort. As a matter of fact, I haven't even heard one of them speak."

"Don't beat around the bush, general, ask what's on your mind," Harry told him. "I'll give you an answer if I have one."

"Do you believe this Indian can travel in the Spirit World like you?" he asked.

"You know the answer to that question, general, you know he can," Harry told him. "I know you sensed that when we were talking to Eyes into the future and finding out Many Lives was his son, we have to believe he can."

"Then, do you think he is waiting for us?" the general asked. "Is he in there setting up his trap knowing we are coming and how many of us there are, or is he not aware of our presence and just circling down around the backs of unsuspecting soldiers?"

"I can't answer that question, general. I honestly don't know," and Harry didn't.

"What I can tell you is this. He won't attack us head on. He will launch his arrows into the air so they can rain down on the troops who aren't looking at being attacked from the sky. But, now you know what to be aware of. Have your men watch the sky as well as what's in front of them," is what Harry told him. "Many Lives and his warriors are not bullet proof. Believe me. Hit them, they will die."

The distant echo of gunfire told them they needed to end our conversation and get in there and capture or kill Many Lives and his renegade warriors.

Returning to the troops, General Mathis quickly laid out the plan of attack. When the general finished filling in his men on the plan, Harry informed him that Conrad and he wouldn't be joining him, but would enter behind the great rock formation where they could get above the battlefield and keep watch on the happenings.

"Keep an eye on us, general. Use your field glasses, that way I can give you hand signals as to where Many Lives warriors are located," they agreed, and all his troops made preparations for the impending battle.

Conrad and Harry headed towards the great rock formation. As they reached the backside of the rock formation, they heard several volleys of rifle fire.

"It would appear the general's plan has begun," Harry whispered to Conrad.

If all went to plan, the soldiers he was sending in to combine forces with Lieutenant Hasting's had taken place and they had succeeded in overtaking however many warriors were confronting them. The plan now was to join together and continue around the flat ridge where it is believed Many Lives and the remainder of his warriors were circling around to attack the lieutenant from the rear. If all goes to plan, Many Lives and his warriors will be trapped between the two.

Once Harry and Conrad reached the top of the rock formation they had a view of the whole area, and although far away, easily made out the forms of the soldiers as they moved about. But no Indians were spotted.

As suspected, the first part of the plan must have gone off as they thought. Looking at the area directly below where the lieutenant and his men were held down, it was now empty. Gone were all of the soldiers. What they did see were three dead Indians placed out in the open so Harry would know that part of the plan was successful.

Suddenly, a lot of gunfire was heard and turning in its direction Harry was able to see the general and his men had left their mounts and had taken cover behind rocks and trees and were firing directly in front of them into the area where Harry and the general figured Many Lives would be headed if he was indeed circling around to attack from the rear.

Harry scanned the area looking for any movement by Many Lives or his warriors and saw none. The only movement was those of General Mathis and those of Lieutenant Hastings soldiers.

Not seeing Many Lives, Harry stood up so the general could see me. Knowing he was looking at Harry through field glasses, Harry shrugged his shoulders and mouthed the words, "they're gone."

"Where did they go Harry?" asked Conrad. "They couldn't just disappear, could they?"

There had to be a good answer to that question.

"Of course they didn't disappear," Harry told him. "There has to be a cave or something where they could hide so well they couldn't be seen."

"Is it possible for them to enter the Spirit World and vanish?" Conrad questioned.

"No they couldn't. The Spirit World is for spirits, not human flesh," Harry told Conrad. "You can enter as the spirit of whatever animal you choose, but in spirit form only."

When Harry saw the general and his troops emerge out into the open, Harry told Conrad it was time to go down there and look around. By the time they reached

General Mathis, Lieutenant Hastings' men were also gathered there.

"Where did the Indians disappear to?" Harry asked, riding up to the two commanders who had joined together in conversation.

"We don't know. One minute I saw a couple of them right where we thought they would be and we fired rounds at them, and the next minute they were gone," said the general. "Then we met up with the lieutenant's men."

"Why haven't you searched the area for them," Harry asked them both. "You know they couldn't just vanish into thin air."

"I figured we would make camp here and get some food going and search the area at the same time," said the general.

Already, Harry saw four of the general's men were busy gathering wood and building a fire. Others were busy emptying sacks of canned goods which they opened, emptying them together in a large pot sitting in the fire.

Harry noticed the lieutenant's men watching them.

"Looks like your men don't quite know what to make of the general's colored soldiers," Harry said to the lieutenant low enough not to be heard by any of the troops.

"We have all heard of the general's Buffalo Soldiers, but have never been face to face with them until now. And as you can see, my men are thirsty and hungry but make no move to mingle with them, nor do the colored soldiers offer an invite for them to do so."

All the while, General Mathis listened to our conversation, once he sensed we were done he then spoke up.

"Let me shed some light on your conversation now you two have had your say," General Mathis spoke up.

"My men have orders not to mingle with any other soldier who aren't of their skin color unless they are approached first. We used to be a very friendly troop, until we were treated differently by the white soldiers, now we stay to ourselves. All your men have to do, lieutenant, is to walk over to any of my men and offer up friendship and you will see. But you won't get the invite first."

When he had finished, the lieutenant walked away to join his men. Harry watched the lieutenant gather his men together and talked to them. Several times Harry watched as one or two of the lieutenant's men looked over at the general's men as they went about getting a stew of some kind made.

Soon the lieutenant turned from his men and started to walk towards the general's men. He was soon followed by his men, and together they started to mingle with the colored soldiers. Shortly after, you could hear laughter and the all-around sound of comradery between the men.

"Well, what do you make of that general," Harry asked after several minutes.

"I'd say that thirst and hunger will make a man do just about anything," the general replied with a small chuckle.

"I would agree, general," Harry said, "now let's go and see if your men will share some of that coffee I smell."

Once the men were done and their utensils washed and packed away, it was time to see if we could find out where Many Lives vanished to.

"Look for any boulder that might seem out of place because it could be covering over the entrance to a cave," Harry instructed the men. "Keep your eyes up also just in case Many Lives has something different in store for us."

"Look for tracks, also," the lieutenant told his men. "Anything that is out of place."

"Anyone have any questions before we start?" Harry asked "If not, let's go."

The opening was so narrow you would have missed it if you weren't looking for it, plus it was the only thing they had discovered.

"Corporal. Go and bring Hagar here right now," General Mathis instructed one of his soldiers.

Minutes later he returned with one of the general's Indian scouts named Hagar.

Hagar was instructed to work his way through the narrow gap to see where it led to.

About a half hour passed before Hagar returned. When he did it wasn't through the gap, but right behind us. Turns out the gap went on for about two hundred yards then emptied into a large rocky area which was tree lined and would make for an easy unseen escape.

Foot prints in the area told Harry this was where Many Lives had vanished. The plans were for the lieutenant to take his troops back to Fort Kearney and the general would try to follow Many Lives' tracks.

Conrad and Harry decided to go their own way as Harry was pretty sure he knew where Many Lives was headed and a bunch of Buffalo Soldiers riding back onto the Indian reservation at Two Pines wasn't going to be well received.

Harry couldn't explain why he felt Many Lives would go to the reservation, but something was nagging at him, and like the hairs rising up on his neck as a warning sign he had learned to listen to, the nagging he had learned to follow. The prisons and cemeteries lay claim to the accuracy of his following this nagging he was feeling now.

Harry couldn't explain the feeling to Conrad, who Harry knew well enough to sense Conrad's questions, but also his loyalty to the badge he wore, and Harry's leadership.

As the sky darkened the glow of the campfire created a protective halo over the soldiers. Soon, the humming of the black soldiers filled the heavens as they lifted their voices into the night remembering the tune from some childhood ballad their mamas used to sing for them as she rocked them to sleep.

Tomorrow, they would part ways and probably never see each other again, but they all would carry this moment in their memories. As the night sky got blacker, Harry's eye lids grew heavier, and soon, once again he was hot on the trail of Many Lives.

Chapter 10

It was hard for Harry to distinguish the real world from the Spirit World as he continued his pursuit of Many Lives in his dreams.

Harry was once again a great eagle soaring over the massive plains of the west.

He saw many buffalo herds consisting of thousands of buffalo whose mass numbers seemed to turn the plush green land into a sea of black, moving ever so slowly across the plains, a beauty all its own.

Where are those herds today? he thought. *Gone by the way of the white man's bullets, that's where they are gone*, he thought. *No wonder the Indian hated the white settlers so much.*

Catching some other movement, Harry speeded in its direction. A few powerful flaps of his wings and he was circling above a small band of Indians sitting around a fire. It was Many Lives and they were bedded down for the night.

As the first golden rays of sunlight gave birth to the plains as a new day, Harry was once again soaring through the heavens following the small band of renegade Indians lead by Many Lives, as they raced across the land.

Two days and nights passed and Many Lives was still riding across the plains.

Where are you going? Harry thought.

Suddenly, the sky opened up in front of him and a glowing figure stood there. Harry saw this figure raise both hands into the air. When he did, Harry was no longer an eagle but himself, standing next to this figure.

As the brightness subsided, Harry saw this figure was the Spiritual Leader, Eyes Into the Future and Many Lives' father.

"You ask, where my son is headed. Even though I know what you must do, I also know I want peace between my people and the white man, and as long as there are bands of warrior Indians causing more death to the white settlers, the peace I desire will not come about," he said to Harry. "You must stop him."

"Where is your son headed?" Harry asked "He has been riding long and hard and I don't recognize the land."

"My son travels to the place he killed his first white settlers. He must not reach that place," he told me. "You have to stop him."

"What will happen if I don't?" Harry asked.

"He will receive powers so great he will never be stopped and many, many, more settlers will die," sadness overtook this great Indians face. "You will have to kill him."

"I don't understand," Harry told him.

"My son travels in the evil realms of the Spirit World. He gains in strength and power every time he takes a white man's scalp."

"What does that have to do with returning to the first killings?" Harry asked.

"He raped a white woman there he thought he had killed. He had not. She lived and bore his child. He has learned of this child and now must go and kill his son so he can retain all his powers. If not, he has to bestow them on his son. He will not want to give his powers to his half breed son, so you must stop him."

Having said that, the sky closed with a loud clap of thunder.

"What the heck was that," Harry screamed, having been awakened from a sound sleep by the incoming thunder storm.

"Just some thunder, Harry. Looks like we're gonna get wet."

"I saw him," Harry told Conrad. "I know where he is headed."

Scrambling to find cover from the incoming storm Harry told Conrad of his dream.

"So, Harry. How do we find out exactly where his first raid took place?" asked Conrad.

"Not sure, but he was headed west and several days had passed and still we hadn't arrived at the place he wanted to get to."

"What's your plan, Harry?" asked Conrad. "I know you have one."

"We need to get on a train headed west as soon as we can. We can't overtake them on horseback, but we can if we can travel during the nights, plus we can travel more than twice the distance he can in a day. Let's ride hard back to Dusty Hollow where we can get a train and I can telegraph Fort Kearney again. Someone there might be able to recall an Indian report of a raid where a woman survived the attack."

It was a hard ride and it took its toll on Conrad's leg. The red blood stain that came through his pants told them he was bleeding through his bandages, but he didn't complain. They made it to Dusty Hollow half a day before the train was due.

Harry brought Conrad to the doctor's office and dropped him off and went to see Mandy and told her he was there.

Next, Harry returned to his rail car, made arrangements to have it hitched on when the train arrived, made coffee, and telegraphed Fort Kearney.

A telegraph back from Fort Kearney and Harry had the information he was looking for.

The US Government had required the commanders at any fort to document all Indian activity. The Harris Ranch was the one Harry was seeking. A white woman, Mary Harris had survived, and was still on the ranch, refusing to be driven off. The ranch was outside of Ogallala a town the train serviced direct.

There was no one at the fort who could authorize troops to go to the Harris Ranch until Lieutenant Hastings returned.

As the train pulled into the station, Harry's door opened and Conrad entered.

"Well, I was just going to find you. How's the leg?" Harry asked.

"Good. Doc said I tore out a couple of stitches, but no infection."

"That's good news," Harry said. "Do you have any pain?"

"No I don't, Harry. After the doc stitched me back up he put some salve on it that took all the pain out. Almost as good as new," Conrad told me.

"You will have another day and a half to heal more," Harry told him. "Ogallala is about a day and a half train ride from here."

"Do you know much about Ogallala?" Harry asked him.

"Just what you read from time to time. Just another cowboy town."

"Were you able to learn anything new about the Spirit World, Harry, when you saw Eyes Into the Future?"

"Just that his son travels in the Spirit World, but as an evil spirit."

The train arrived and they were hitched up and left the station on schedule. The train trip to Ogallala was uneventful. No dreams captivated Harry's nights.

It would appear Harry was armed with everything he would need to defeat Many Lives when the time came.

In Ogallala, Conrad and Harry rented two horses for the remainder of the trip to the Harris Ranch, which was about five miles out of town.

Before they left, they stopped into the sheriff's office to introduce themselves and to advise him of their assignment.

"Why don't you two go over to The Rose Garden and get some food or coffee and I will meet you there in ten minutes. I'm going with you," he said. "I'll get my deputy and meet you there."

Sheriff Franks was gone before Harry had time to object.

Having a couple more guns if Many Lives has his warriors would be a welcomed addition, Harry thought.

Harry and Conrad chose pie and coffee while they waited for the sheriff and deputy who arrived some ten minutes later.

"This here is William Day, we all just call him Willie. Willie is my deputy," he told them.

With introductions out of the way, and they didn't want anything, it was time to go.

As they rode, Harry told the sheriff all he knew about Many Lives, but the sheriff had already heard some of the stories, and there was a time he went after him but had lost track of him and gave up his pursuit.

Harry chose not to mention the supernatural or the Spirit World to Sheriff Franks.

"What makes you so sure he is on his way here," asked Sheriff Franks. "I don't understand."

"It's a long story and I'll share everything with you later, but for now we must ride hard because I'm not sure exactly when he might show up."

Arriving at the Harris Ranch right at dusk, Harry wasn't sure how they were going to be greeted, but it turned out Mary was a very independent woman, and she welcomed them into her home.

"Would anyone like coffee or something to eat?" she asked. "And then you can tell me what you are doing here."

"What makes you so sure he's on his way here?" she asked Harry.

"We were on the reservation where his father lives and he wants peace between his people and the white man. He knows that won't happen as long as his son continues his raiding and killing of settlers," Harry told her.

"But why come here? I still don't understand."

Deciding Harry needed to tell her the truth, he began his story by telling her who Many Lives' father is.

"His father is also the Spiritual Leader of the people and has special powers, he is able to look into the future. He told me his son was headed here because you have his son."

There. I said it. Let's see what happens next. Harry thought.

Silence followed. Minutes passed before Mary got up from her chair and walked to the door. Leaning against the door frame and staring out into the dark of the evening, she started to talk.

There were no tears as she told of watching everyone killed by the raiding party that day. No tears as she told of the hours she was repeatedly raped, and then stabbed in the chest and thought dead, her scalp cut from her head.

When she was finished, she turned back to Harry and repeated her earlier question.

"So. Is he coming here to claim his son?" she asked. "Well, he's not going to get him. I'll kill him first."

"You won't have to Mary. That's why we're here," Harry told her. "What I don't know is when exactly and how many warriors he will have with him. If it is okay, I want us to hang out in the barn and wait for him."

Harry secretly hoped the old saying of good always wins over evil was true. The night went by without any visits. As the sun came up, Harry got his group together and told them to go back to town as he was pretty sure Many Lives would wait until dark to show up, even if he arrived during the day.

"Be back early afternoon though," he told them as they rode off.

Having been awake all night, Harry told Conrad he was going to get some shut eye. The nagging in his gut told him tonight was going to be the night. Having slept most of the afternoon, as evening came upon the Harris Ranch, Harry was wide awake.

The sheriff and his deputy had returned and were in the hay loft. Conrad and Harry had taken up locations in the front and rear of the barn giving them a view of the front and rear of the ranch home.

Mary, as instructed, had put the child to bed early and sat in her lighted living room with a cocked Colt in her lap, hidden by a wrap.

The night air was hot and deadly quiet. Plans were that no one was to enter the house. A slight clacking of the tongue was the signal that Indians were approaching. From there, it was at their discretion when to fire.

The hairs started rising on the back of Harry's neck as a warning just before they heard the "yip, yip" echo into the quietness of the night. This was a familiar signal that the Indians used and Harry was sure all heard it and now were alerted to Many Lives' arrival.

Harry had hoped that with sleep that day, he would also visit the Spirit World so that Harry would know what was about to take place, but Many Lives had not, so Harry was on his own.

As Harry's eyes scanned the darkness, his ears picked up a strange sound which was getting louder and louder. It sounded just like a mother's lips when she held her finger up to them and gave you a shhhhhhhhhhhhhh sound to be quiet.

This followed by a loud, resounding, thuddddd as the arrow sank its tip into the wood right above Harry's head. Looking up where the arrow hit, he caught sight of the three red bands painted on its center.

At the same instant, several shots were heard from the rear of the barn, these followed by the loud cry of someone being hit.

Where is the moon light when you need it? thought Harry, as he scanned the darkness looking to pick up some movement.

As if someone had heard his request, the darkness was suddenly lighted as the blackened sky gave up its moonlight. Looking up, Harry didn't see the moon, instead he saw the face of Eyes Into the Future. Movement to his left indicated the presence of incoming danger, but before he could react, Conrad did.

A scream of pain and another one of Many Lives' renegades were down.

Now that the landscape was lighted up, Harry could make out the forms of five dead Indians.

That leaves only two warriors plus Many Lives, were Harry's thoughts, as he tried to sum up where they stood.

Another movement and a lone Indian was seen half running, half limping across the front yard head for the front door of the ranch house. Instantly, out of pure reflex, Harry's rifle came up and two well placed rounds of lead entered into his chest, dropped him in his tracks.

"Are you boys okay?" Harry whispered, loud enough to be heard.

"We're all okay, Harry," came his answer. "How many do you figure are left out there?"

"Providing he only had the same number he was noted as having, there are only two left. Is one of them Many Lives? I would bet on it."

"What will he do now, Harry?" Conrad questioned.

"There's only one way to answer that question," Harry replied.

It all had to end here and now. It was my assignment to see to it that happened, and that's what I will do. Harry thought

Remembering the broken arrows and their meaning, Harry leaned his rifle against the barn door casing and stepped out into the front yard.

"Harry, Harry," he heard Conrad call out. "Harry, what are you doing?" Harry could hear the alarm in his voice, but at the same time, Harry heard Conrad cock his rifle in readiness. Out of nowhere a screaming Indian came charging at Harry with a knife held high above his head, the last of Many Lives' renegades.

BOOOOOM, roared Conrad's Springfield stopping the racing Indian in his tracks. A cloud of dust rising into the air as his dead form hit the dirt.

"Many Lives," Harry called out, not knowing for certain he was alive or dead, but was staking his life there was only one Indian left.

The moon was abruptly darkened for a few seconds before it showed its silvery face again.

"White man, I told you we would meet again."

To Harry's amazement, an Indian was standing there, right in front of him.

The painted face, the many eagle feathers in his hair, the shield of scalps that covered his chest, all telling Harry he was standing there face to face with Many Lives.

"You know what I come for, white man. We can have a peace between us. My warriors are dead. I want my son."

"Your father has warned me against you taking the boy. I will not let that happen," Harry told him.

"My father, I will take care of him on the other side," he said. Both of them knowing what he was saying.

"Then one of us must die," he said, taking off the armor of scalps and dropping them to the ground.

A knife appeared in his hand and he flung his body towards Harry. He side-stepped his advance and for the next five minutes they were locked together in hand to hand combat.

Many Lives was strong and soon Harry grew weary, but Harry knew that he mustn't show weakness or the fight would be over and his scalp would join the others Many Lives wore so proudly around his neck.

Harry knew Many Lives could sense him weakening, just by the look in his eye and the slight smile that came over his face. As he straddled Harry's prone body with his knife barely inches from Harry's chest, his hands were grasped in Harry's and he was holding the knife back.

It's said, when you are close to death your whole life flashes before your eyes, no truer words were ever spoken. Taking shape in a smoke cloud right above Many Lives' head was Harry's life in pictures. From birth to right now, they were there for him to re-live for an instant.

And then, through the pictures and the smoke cloud, Harry caught sight of the moon, once again he saw the face of Eyes Into the Future. This time, Harry saw a tear form at the corner of one eye then flooded over and rolled down his cheek.

Eyes Into the Future words came back to Harry loud and clear. "He must not live."

Harry didn't know where his strength came from, but he stopped the downward course of Many Lives' knife and with all the strength left in Harry, pushed the knife forward and upward slicing into Many Lives' stomach and cutting all the way to his ribs.

Harry was aware of something hot covering his front side. Looking down, it was Many Lives blood and innards. A gurgling sound escaped Many Lives' lips.

Looking down at Harry, he said, "Yadalanh Ka Dish Day."

"No, we won't meet again," Harry whispered back, then pulled the knife out and plunged it deep in the center of his chest, piercing his heart.

Harry couldn't explain it, but as the life left Many Lives, Harry felt it wanting to enter his, but Harry sensed it was the evil power from the Spirit World and Harry called upon his very being to overcome this new onslaught of evil. Then as quickly as it had come about, it was gone.

The reign of Many Lives and his band of renegades ended there that night, and Harry secretly prayed it would be his last encounter with Indians and the Spirit World.

Epilogue

Even though Many Lives had caused much disgrace for his father, Harry was sure Eyes Into the Future would like his son's body, so he could give him the proper Apache burial. It was for this reason Harry transported Many Lives body back to the reservation at Two Pines and to his father. The look on his father's face, Harry will remember always.

He spent a couple of days in Dusty Hollow with Conrad finishing up all the paperwork needed to close this assignment. In his trophy case, Harry added two oversized long arrows with three red rings painted around their centers.

Not in Harry's trophy case, but in the trunk where he kept other items, was the crisscross gun belts with all the scalps Many Lives had removed himself, all except one. That one was Mary's. She asked if she could have it and Harry told her yes.

When she removed it from the gun belt, there were tears in her eyes.

What was she remembering? The killing of her family? The rape she underwent by the band of savages? The painful removing of her scalp while still alive? Harry thought. It was hard to think which one, other than them all.

This time also gave Conrad a little time to spend with Mandy, who at the end of the two days he had fallen in love with, and asked her to marry him. The question she answered yes to.

Asking Harry's advice on what he should do, Harry told him, but also said it had to be their decisions. "You have been given a territory to manage and I think Mandy needs to sell off her place and move to your location. She can buy another eatery or saloon, or a boarding house."

Conrad and Mandy would get married. Mandy would sell and move to be with her husband. Conrad would go on to be a much decorated US Marshal and their trails would cross many times in the future.

Harry wanted nothing more than to return to his Amanda and soon to be family, and a cup of steaming, black coffee.